THE
DEADLY
GAME

THE MALICHEA QUEST

Also by Jim Elridge

The Invisible Assassin

THE DEADLY GAME

THE MALICHEA QUEST

JIM ELDRIDGE

BLOOMSBURY

LONDON NEW DELHI NEW YORK SYDNEY

Bloomsbury Publishing, London, New Delhi, New York and Sydney

First published in Great Britain in September 2012 by
Bloomsbury Publishing Plc
50 Bedford Square, London, WC1B 3DP

A CIP catalogue record for this book is available from the British Library

ISBN 978 1 4088 1720 9

Typeset by Hewer Text UK Ltd, Edinburgh
Printed in Great Britain by Clays Ltd, St Ives Plc, Bungay, Suffolk

1 3 5 7 9 10 8 6 4 2

www.bloomsbury.com
www.jimeldridge.com

For Lynne, for ever

The screams came from the man tied to the chair in the middle of the room. He'd been screaming for hours, in between sobbing and pleading for the torture to stop. There were two other men in the room. One was tall and muscular, with the broken nose of a boxer. The other, small and wiry, was holding something metal in his hand that glistened with blood. Both men looked on impassively, although the shorter man's face seemed to show a hint of a smile. The man in the chair suddenly slumped forward, his blood-soaked body straining against the ropes that held him. Boxer frowned and ran his fingers down the side of the tortured man's neck, feeling for a pulse. Then he switched to the wrist, the tips of his fingers searching for a sign of life beneath the flayed skin of the man's arm.

He looked up and shook his head. 'He's dead,' he said.

1

The short man scowled. Just then his mobile phone rang. He pressed the phone to his ear, and then said abruptly: 'No, he ain't talked.' He cast a look of annoyance at the body strapped in the chair and added: 'And he ain't likely to any more.'

He listened some more, then hung up. He turned to Boxer. 'He says forget about him. He's got another job for us.'

Boxer gestured towards the lifeless body. 'What about him?' he asked.

The short man gave an evil grin.

'One for the pigs,' he said.

Chapter 1

Jake Wells sat in front of his computer and smiled into his webcam, beaming at the face looking back at him from his screen. Lauren Graham. Fugitive, exile, killer; his girlfriend.

He looked at the clock. 11 p.m. here in the UK. 11 a.m. in Wellington, New Zealand. In the old days people had to content themselves with intercontinental phone calls and echoing time delays. But now, with Skype, they could see one another, even though they were on opposite sides of the globe.

It was three months ago that Lauren had boarded a plane for New Zealand to start a new life with a new identity. Samantha Adams. That was what it said on her passport, her birth certificate and all the other documents MI5 had provided for her. But to Jake, she would always be Lauren.

'I went on a trip to South Island the other week,' she said. 'We went to the Franz Josef Glacier. It's amazing.

3

It runs down to rainforest — two totally contrasting climates right next to each other . . .'

'We?' Jake said, his heart sinking. Had she met someone else?

Lauren laughed.

'Me and a girl from work,' she reassured him, sensing his discomfort. 'She's really nice. Her name's Anna. She works with me at the research centre.'

The Antarctic Survey Research Centre, where Lauren — or rather, Sam Adams — had found a job studying environmental information from the base stations all over Antarctica.

Jake smiled.

'I've been doing some exploring, too,' he told her. 'Last week I went for a stroll at a place called Firle Beacon . . .'

There was a pinging sound from the screen, and suddenly the image of Lauren vanished. In its place a message appeared: *An error has occurred. This programme will close*. And then, as Jake watched, one by one the logos on the screen disappeared and finally the screen went blank. His computer had shut down.

He pressed the keys to reboot it. While it was starting up, he picked up his landline phone and dialled Lauren's mobile number. He got an automated message telling him: 'The mobile you are trying to call is unavailable. Please try later.'

He cursed. Lauren's mobile wasn't switched off. They'd been cut off deliberately. It had happened a lot when she had first been in New Zealand, but they'd learned that it was always when they started talking about Malichea and the hidden books. So they'd been more careful, and for quite a while they'd only discussed day-to-day things, where they'd been, what movies they'd seen.

Sometimes he'd be silly and romantic, holding up a single red rose towards the camera and then feeling happiness pour through him as she blew him a kiss and told him how much she wished they could be together again.

'We will be,' he promised her.

He didn't know how, there were so many obstacles to overcome, but he knew they were destined to be together. He needed her properly in his life — not just a moving image of her on a computer screen.

He tried phoning her again, but the connection was still broken.

He sighed and sent her an email, and hoped they'd at least allow this through to her . . .

Chapter 2

Next morning, Jake arrived at the Department of Science building in London's Whitehall district; the heart of government. As a working-class young man of nineteen, Jake was an anomaly in this place. Everyone else here, especially in the Press Office where he worked, seemed to have come through the same route: public school, then university, mostly Oxford or Cambridge. Jake was different. Eighteen months before a national newspaper had pointed out how elitist this was, and the department had acted to prove them wrong: a competition had been launched to offer an opportunity for a trainee press officer from what was termed 'the disadvantaged'. Jake had entered. He fitted the bill perfectly: abandoned at birth, brought up in a children's home and then a string of foster homes, and left school at sixteen because he couldn't afford to go on to further education. After he left school he worked in a series of dead-end jobs. But he always had one burning ambition: to be a journalist. He wanted to write witty and biting articles about the issues of the day, expose corrupt politicians. But getting into journalism wasn't that easy; he discovered that he needed a degree.

It was while he had been wondering how to get over this problem that he'd read about the Department of Science competition, entered it, and won his place. That had been a year ago. At that time everything had seemed exciting, a life and a career full of possibilities.

And then the hidden books of Malichea had come into his life, and everything had been turned upside down.

He knew what lay ahead for him this morning: there'd be a message for him to go and see the head of the department, Gareth Findlay-Weston, and then a dressing down from Gareth for breaking the rules. But he *hadn't* broken any rules. All he'd done was talked to his girlfriend and told her what he'd been doing. All right, privately he admitted to himself, there had been more to it than that. Each time he and Lauren talked, they tried to find a coded way of talking about the Order of Malichea and the hidden books, without the people who were listening in and

7

watching them, picking up on it. So far they hadn't succeeded. But Jake had thought this time he'd found a way: an uncontroversial chat about a walk he'd been on in the Sussex countryside. He'd hoped that Lauren might read between the lines; that he'd been through her list of possible hiding places for the hidden library, and was checking one of them out: a long ancient barrow at West Firle. This first visit he'd made had been to recce the site for a possible dig later, perhaps under cover of darkness, but the size of the site had given him doubts. He needed to narrow down his area of search in some way. Right now, he wasn't sure how, but the place was a definite possible.

Jake walked into the large open-plan office where the department press office was based. It was just after nine o'clock, and already everyone seemed to be at their phones or their computer terminals, chasing down stories or responding to press requests. As Jake got to his desk, his fellow press officer, Paul Evans, hung up from a phone call and greeted Jake with a cheery grin.

'What time do you call this?' he demanded.

Jake looked at his watch.

'I call it five past nine,' he said. 'Why?'

'You should have been here at nine,' said Paul.

'My bus got stuck in traffic,' said Jake.

'You should use a bike, like I do,' said Paul. 'It's better for the environment, and gets through traffic quicker than anything else.'

'Yeah, and you get lungfuls of diesel fumes and you're liable to get knocked off it by some crazy driver,' pointed out Jake.

Paul shook his head.

'Not if you're careful,' he said. 'Also, I wear a filter mask to protect against fumes. Trust me, Jake, you'd be a lot healthier if you biked it to work.'

Jake looked at him suspiciously.

'Are you involved in some sort of government press initiative to get everyone in London cycling?' he asked.

Paul looked slightly uncomfortable.

'Maybe,' he said. 'Although it's just in the planning stage at the moment. Anyway, Gareth was looking for you.'

Jake's heart sank. As he'd feared.

'When?' he asked.

'He was waiting by your desk when I came in dead at nine,' said Paul. 'That's why I said you should have been here on time. It doesn't do to upset the big boss.'

'What did he want?' asked Jake.

'He wanted to know if you were in. I covered for you, told him you were most likely in the toilet, but I'm not sure if he believed me.'

Unlikely, thought Jake. Gareth never believed anyone about anything. That was why he was so good at the job he did. Officially, Gareth was head of the press office at the Department of Science. Behind the scenes, he was a very senior MI5 spook, with the power of life and death over people. People like Lauren and Jake. But, as far as Jake was aware, he was the only one in his department who knew about Gareth's real role. And he knew his life, and Lauren's, were at stake if he breathed a word to anyone about it.

'I'd better pop up and see him,' said Jake.

Just then, Paul's phone rang, and he was soon engaged in a conversation that appeared to be about how exercising the legs increased the supply of oxygen to the lungs and brain. Yes, Paul was definitely on a 'cycling is good for you' story.

With a sense of foreboding, Jake left the large office and began to mount the wide staircase to the third floor, and Gareth's sanctuary. As always, he noticed the change to the decor as he went higher. From the ground floor to the second, everything was hi-tech, thrusting modern. Then, as you left what could loosely be called the 'public' areas and entered the upper echelons, where the real power lay, the world changed, slipping back in time a hundred years or more. The banisters changed from ordinary metal to brass. The light fittings, which were plain white plastic up to the second floor, became shining gun-metal.

As Jake walked along the narrow corridor, panelled with dark oak, the wood adorned with old paintings showing an England long past, hunting scenes, countryside celebrations, his sense of dread was replaced with one of anger. Yes, he knew that Gareth was going to look at him and sigh with that tone of unhappy resignation Gareth did so well, and then proceed to tear him to shreds with his caustic, sarcastic language, which was not a happy experience. But what right did Gareth have? thought Jake indignantly. Jake hadn't been doing anything wrong. Well, not on the face of it. Even if Gareth suspected that Jake was trying to pass on some information to Lauren about the books, there was no proof. Not this time, anyway. And Gareth had had a nerve to shut down the Skype connection between him and Lauren. Well, Jake would have something to say about that!

Jake arrived at the door to Gareth's office, knocked, and went in to be met by Gareth's assistant, Janet.

'He's ready for you,' said Janet, and she ushered Jake smartly over to an inner office. Gareth was sitting behind his huge desk, empty except for a few papers, on which he was scribbling some annotations. He looked up as Jake arrived, and the inner door closed behind Janet.

Gareth gave an unhappy sigh.

'What are we going to do with you, Jake?' he asked in a tone that showed his deep disappointment.

Jake said nothing, just waited for the dressing-down he knew was coming, and got ready to bark back.

'I thought we had an agreement,' continued Gareth. 'That you and Ms Graham would forget about the secret library of Malichea.'

'No,' Jake corrected him. 'Our agreement was that we wouldn't *search* for any more of the books.'

Gareth regarded Jake with his standard bland expression, but Jake could see the steel in his eyes, and now that same icy hardness entered Gareth's voice as he said flatly: 'Don't mess with me, Jake. We could have put your girlfriend on trial for murder, but we didn't, because we wanted to give both of you a chance at a fresh start.'

'Her in New Zealand and me over here, and not allowed to meet, is hardly how I would describe a fresh start.'

'Separately, Jake. It has to be separately,' said Gareth. 'We both know why.'

'Yes, but I'm sure you're going to tell me, anyway.'

'To remind you.' Now it was Gareth's turn to do the correcting. 'Apart, on opposite sides of the planet, you're not a danger. When you get together, insane ideas seem to take on some kind of reality for you both.'

'All we wanted to do was put the library into the public domain. Let the people know about the texts. What they contain. How they can help people.'

Gareth shook his head, wearing his more-in-sadness-than-in-anger expression again.

'They won't help people, Jake. Not the kind of people you're talking about. The only people who will benefit are gangsters, warmongers, terrorists, patents lawyers.' He shook his head sorrowfully again. 'I thought you'd accepted that. But obviously, you haven't.'

'You shut down our Skype call yesterday,' said Jake, doing his best to control his anger.

Gareth shook his head.

'An automatic safeguard in the system shut it down,' he said. 'Obviously, we then got an alert to tell us what had happened, and a playback of your conversation.'

'We didn't mention the word Malichea,' said Jake. 'Or anything about the books.'

Gareth looked down at a print-out on his desk. Looking at it upside down, Jake saw that it appeared to be a script. He assumed it was the transcript of his and Lauren's Skype call.

'You said: "I went for a stroll at a place called Firle Beacon",' read Gareth.

'Well, I did,' said Jake, annoyed. 'So what? That's what you do when you talk to friends, you tell them what you've been up to. Things you've done. Interesting

13

places you've been. I thought it might cheer Lauren up, remind her of England.'

Gareth didn't bother to look up. He took a sheet of paper from a small pile at one side of his desk, and read aloud: 'Firle Beacon, West Firle, East Sussex. Said to be the burial place of a giant.' He looked up at Jake. 'In other words, one of the list of places that is said to be sacred, cursed or haunted. According to your very own Ms Graham, the very place that one of the Malichea texts might have been hidden.'

'I wasn't looking for any of the books,' defended Jake. He was lying, of course. And he could tell that Gareth knew it.

'Jake, I would have thought you would have been aware of it by now, the number of times you have been cut off when talking to Ms Graham; but in case you haven't yet worked it out: in addition to the security system being programmed with the name Malichea, and every other possible permutation that may be used to describe either the Order of Malichea, or the library, or the abbots or monks of the Order, it also contains every place in the British Isles that fits with the definition of sacred, cursed or haunted. It is also programmed with the list of the author and name of every suspected title believed to have been hidden by the Order. Any of those words can trigger the cut-off of any Skype conversation, email, or phone call, and a report will then be automatically generated and delivered to me.' He looked Jake directly in the eyes. 'Do you understand what I'm saying, Jake?'

Yes, thought Jake. If you even think we might be talking about the secret library, we'll get cut off. And as he and Lauren had discovered that their letters were also being opened and read, and censored, the powers-that-be were making absolutely sure that Jake and Lauren would never again be able to even hint at mentioning the forbidden books.

'Pierce Randall are still looking for the books,' blurted out Jake.

Pierce Randall, the powerful international legal firm, with a client list that included dictators, organised crime around the globe, as well as governments and multinational companies.

Gareth hesitated, then he nodded slightly. 'We are dealing with Pierce Randall,' he said. 'They know the rules of the game. At this moment, you are the wild card, the unstable element. I hope I don't need to remind you that unstable elements cannot be tolerated in an orderly world.'

In other words, stop or we'll kill you. You and Lauren, thought Jake in horror as he decoded Gareth's outwardly bland words. It would be done in an untraceable manner. An unfortunate and tragic accident.

'Do I make myself clear?' asked Gareth.

Jake hesitated, then he nodded.

'Yes,' he said.

Gareth's happy smile returned to his face.

'Good,' he purred. 'Then we have an understanding?'

'Yes.' Jake nodded again.

Chapter 3

Jake caught the bus home. It was crowded and slower than the tube, but after his experience a few months ago, when a would-be assassin had almost succeeded in pushing him under a tube train, he felt safer. He still didn't know who had been behind that attempt on his life. He suspected Gareth's secret service people, but it didn't make sense. Not now, now that Gareth knew about Jake's interests in the secret library, and Jake knew about Gareth being the person responsible for keeping the books hidden and the truth about them hushed up.

He thought about Lauren, far away in New Zealand, exiled. Never able to return. Unless he could find a way to force the government to change their mind. And there was only one way to get them to do that, and that was to get the whole business of the Order of Malichea and the books out into the public arena. End the secrecy. Once it was out in the open, they wouldn't have the same hold over Lauren. OK, there was the murder charge. But Jake still felt that was a bluff. For one thing, it wasn't murder, Lauren had killed Parsons in self-defence. For another, if they prosecuted her, it would bring out a lot of stuff they'd prefer to keep hidden: like the secret experiments at the government research laboratory from where Jake and Lauren had taken the one book he'd seen.

Jake thought about contacting Pierce Randall, offering to work with them. They had at least one of the old books; Alex Munro, the chief executive at Pierce Randall had told Jake so himself. But Jake also knew that Pierce Randall weren't interested in finding the books for 'the common good', as Munro had claimed. The international law firm wanted the books for their clients for the money they would make, for the power they would bring: to be able to hold governments and companies to ransom, to destroy and remake national economics, to use the scientific information as weapons.

No, Pierce Randall would be the wrong direction. They wouldn't help him gain Lauren's freedom.

The bus pulled up at his stop in Finsbury Park, and he walked to the small block of flats where he lived. As he walked, he cast glances around, looking for anyone suspicious, anyone who might be keeping a watch on him. It had become a habit of his, ever since he had become involved with the Order of Malichea.

I have to stop worrying, he told himself. Gareth and his men know about me. They're keeping watch on me. Pierce Randall aren't interested in me if I don't have one of the books. No one's after me. I'm safe.

But he didn't feel it. Sometimes, he thought he'd never feel safe again. That was another reason to get the whole business of the Order of Malichea and the hidden library out into the open. No one would touch him or Lauren once it was out there.

He opened the door of his flat, picked up the mail from the doormat, walked into his kitchen, and stopped dead. A large envelope was lying on his kitchen table. He knew it hadn't been there when he'd left. Someone had been in his flat and put it there. They hadn't broken in, the lock on his front door was undamaged. He looked at the windows. All of them were shut, and locked, exactly as he'd left them. And no one had keys to his flat except him.

He approached the table warily. The envelope looked bulky. It had his name, Jake Wells, printed on it.

Warning bells sounded in his brain. His mind went back to the site in Bedfordshire, when he'd seen that digger driver dig up one of the books, open it, and then the man's whole body had been consumed by a mass of writhing vegetation within seconds. Was there something like that in this envelope? Some booby trap, waiting for him to open it, and fall victim? Jake wondered if he should plunge the envelope into a sink full of water as a safety precaution, just in case. But then he reflected that whatever was inside the envelope might be more dangerous when it came into contact with water.

Of course, he could always throw the envelope away, unopened. But someone had deliberately come into his flat and placed it carefully there for him. And he reasoned, if they wanted to kill him, there were plenty of easier and more straightforward ways to do it.

This was to do with the hidden Malichea books, that was obvious. And any piece of information he could get about them could be a step nearer to freeing Lauren.

Jake picked up the envelope carefully. Whatever was inside it was light. And soft. Nothing hard-edged or rigid. Not metallic. So, hopefully, not a bomb.

Jake opened the flap. It wasn't sealed. Cautiously, he peered into the envelope. There was something thin and dark in there. He upended the envelope, and an object dropped out on to the table. He recognised it straight away: old darkened leather, still soft, dull but with a strange sheen to it where it had been made waterproof. It was the cover of a book, with its pages removed. On its flat surface was the embossed symbol of the Order of Malichea, a capital letter M with a snake coiled through it. And carved into the leather, the Roman numerals CXXI. 121.

It was a protective cover from one of the hidden books, hundreds of years old. And it was book number 121. It was identical in style and material to the book that Jake and Lauren had rescued from the research centre at Hadley Park. That book had been number 367.

Why send me just the cover? thought Jake. Straight away, he knew his question was idiotic. The information in the books was what was valuable. So where was the book? And what was it about?

Jake looked again into the envelope, and saw there was a piece of paper inside. He took it out. On it were typed the words: *Suggest we meet*.

Yes, please, thought Jake. This could be exactly what he needed to get Lauren back to England: one of the books. Proof of the existence of the library.

The sound of his doorbell ringing startled him. He wondered who it could be, he didn't get many callers. Then it struck him that his caller could be the person who'd delivered the cover to him. If so, why didn't they just walk in, like they had before? Perhaps they wanted to play it carefully, not frighten him by just appearing inside his flat unannounced.

The doorbell rang again. Whoever it was, was impatient.

'Coming!' called Jake.

He hurried to the front door, and looked through the spyhole on to the landing. A figure in a courier's yellow top and wearing a crash helmet was standing there, holding a small parcel. Could this be the book itself?

Jake unlocked the door and opened it. As he did so, he was aware of another figure out of the corner of his eye, this one appearing from by the wall of the landing. Then something was sprayed into his eyes. He let out a yell and stumbled back, groping for the door to slam it shut, but before he could do so, they were on him. Strong arms wrapped themselves around him, pinioning his arms to his sides, and then a pad was pressed over his mouth and nose. A sickly smell filled his nose. Chloroform . . . !

Chapter 4

Jake came round. He felt sick. His head felt heavy. He was blindfolded and with a gag over his mouth. For a second, he couldn't work out where he was, he seemed to be suspended. Then he realised he was tied to something with ropes across his chest. He was sitting on a hard chair with his head hanging forward. His hands were tied behind him at the wrists, and his ankles were also tightly bound.

He lifted his head up, and pain flooded through it.

Where am I? he thought. Who's doing this to me? Why?

He strained his ears for movement, trying to work out where his attackers were, but there were no sounds nearby. Maybe he was in one room and they were in another. He tried to work out his location from the acoustics, but there was nothing to help him. No echoes, no noises up close.

He sniffed the air, seeing if he could get any clues that way. Indoor smells. Industrial. Grease, timber and other things he couldn't quite place.

He tried to move, but the chair itself was heavy, and his own weight made it hard to manoeuvre. He attempted to push himself up and bring the chair down on its legs, but he was tied too firmly for that. All that happened was the chair moved a bit, its legs scraping on the ground. But the sound of that scrape was metal on concrete, not wood. And there was a hint of an echo.

He waited, just in case anyone had heard the chair scraping and was coming to him. No one came. He tried again, dragging the chair this time. It only moved a few centimetres, but there was definitely a touch of an echo. He guessed it was a large building with a high roof. The smell of wood and grease suggested it was a warehouse of some kind.

Suddenly he heard a sound. Footsteps in the distance. Careful footsteps. Someone moving cautiously.

They don't want me to hear them coming, he thought. Why? What are they going to do? Creep up on me and hit me to silence me? They must have heard the scrape of the chair.

He stayed still, every nerve and sense now straining to follow the footsteps as they came nearer. Come on, he urged them. Get near enough so I can . . .

So I can what? he thought miserably. I'm tied up so tight I can't move. I can't even fall over on to them.

The footsteps came nearer. Light footsteps, by the sound of it. Soft shoes.

He sat in the chair, waiting for them to get close beside him, tensing himself against the blows he expected to rain down on him.

They were beside him now. He felt something pull at the blindfold . . . and then he was staring into the face of a young woman, who looked at him in astonishment.

'My God!' she said, awed.

Jake stared back at her, his mind a mess of bewilderment. Who was she? And what was she doing here?

He felt a sudden pain as she tore away the tape from over his mouth.

'It's OK,' she said, her tone still one of awe and astonishment. 'I'm a journalist.'

This only made Jake feel even more bewildered.

'A journalist?'

'Yes. My name's Michelle Faure. I had a phone call telling me if I came here I'd find something interesting. I thought it was a crank call, but I'm just starting out, and a story is a story . . .'

As she began to untie the ropes that held his wrists to the chair, she apologised. 'Sorry, I'm gabbling, but I've never been in this situation before. Are you hurt?'

25

'No,' said Jake, his mind still racing. What was a journalist doing here?

As she worked at the knots, he looked around. As he'd guessed, he was in a large warehouse. Timber was stacked around in piles, but it didn't look as if any of it had been moved for some time. There seemed to be a fine layer of dust over everything. The ropes fell away as the knots around his wrists and ankles were finally loosened.

'There!' she said. 'Now we'd better phone your family, let them know you're safe.'

'I don't have any family,' said Jake.

'Well, whoever paid the ransom,' said Michelle.

Jake stared at her.

'What ransom?'

Michelle looked at him, and now it was her turn to look puzzled.

'Well, someone must have paid the ransom, otherwise why did I get the call?'

Jake shook his head.

'Look, I'm not a kidnap victim. Yes, OK, I was grabbed and tied up and left here, but I don't think it was that long ago.' He shot a look at his watch. 'In fact, it only happened about two hours ago.'

'And I got the call twenty minutes ago,' said Michelle. Suddenly her expression changed and she looked at Jake suspiciously. 'Is this some kind of gag?'

'Gag?' echoed Jake indignantly.

'Some sort of practical joke.'

'God, no!' said Jake, heartfelt.

'So, who did it? Did you see them?'

'I saw one of them, he was wearing a sort of courier's uniform and he was holding a parcel.'

'Where was this?'

'Outside my flat. And when I answered the door, this other figure was there, and the next second I had some stuff sprayed in my eyes, and then a pad with chloroform was put over my mouth and nose.'

Michelle still regarded him suspiciously.

'You're sure it's not some kind of joke?'

Jake shook his head.

Michelle fell silent. Then a look of determination entered her eyes.

'We need to phone the police,' she said.

'Why?' asked Jake.

'Why? Because you're a victim of a crime! And a weird crime, at that! Kidnapping for no reason. Assault.' She looked even more determined as she added: 'And I need some kind of police comment, otherwise I don't have much of a story.'

'You don't have a story,' said Jake. 'They let me go unharmed.'

'No,' said Michelle firmly, shaking her head. 'This is obviously a warning of some sort. Gangsters? Drug dealers?' she asked hopefully. 'You've been poking your nose into their business and this is a warning to you.'

'I don't do drugs,' Jake told her, 'and I stay away from people who do.'

Michelle let out a heavy sigh.

'Then why call me to tell me you were here?' she complained.

'I don't know,' said Jake. 'To release me, I suppose.'

'But if that's all it was, why not phone a friend of yours?'

Because I don't have many friends, thought Jake ruefully. 'I don't know.'

Michelle shook her head.

'There has to be a story here,' she said grimly. 'Something I can use.'

And suddenly it hit Jake that this was the opportunity he'd been thinking about for getting the Order of Malichea into the public domain. Getting Lauren's freedom. Of course, he'd have to keep some things back from this woman. Like Lauren killing Carl Parsons. But, if he managed it properly, it could be the answer.

'Actually, Michelle,' he said, 'I think I may have a story for you.'

'And is what's happened here part of it?'

Jake nodded.

'Oh yes,' he said. 'This is definitely part of it.'

Chapter 5

On the promise that Jake would tell her everything that would provide her with a major story, Michelle agreed to drive Jake back to his flat. As it turned out, it wasn't far, the timber storehouse was in an alley off the Holloway Road. Whoever had kidnapped Jake had known the area well enough to know that the timber store was no longer in use, and hadn't been for some time.

Michelle did most of the talking as she drove, and Jake learnt that she was just starting out on her career as a journalist on a magazine called *Qo*.

'It covers everything,' she said. 'News. Fashion. TV. Politics.'

Jake vaguely remembered seeing it on news-stands. Glossy, and usually with a glamorous celebrity on the cover.

'So how does this kidnapping fit in with that?' he asked.

'It's news,' she said.

'Not for a weekly, I'd have thought,' said Jake, still puzzled.

She shrugged as she drove.

'Yes, well, everybody knows it's just a stepping stone for me,' she said. 'What I want to do is get into hard news. Investigative journalism.'

'When you say "everybody" . . . ?'

'Well, not everybody, obviously,' said Michelle. 'Most of the people I work with. Though I've told the editor I see my career as being part of the *Qo* family. No sense in telling him I'd be off like a rocket if the opportunity came up.'

'And you thought discovering a kidnap victim was that opportunity?' asked Jake.

'I didn't know what I'd be discovering,' Michelle reminded him. 'All they said was: "If you go to Patterson Timber Store, you'll find something worthwhile to further your career." That was it.'

'And you went, not knowing what you were going into,' said Jake. 'It could have been anything. A trap. Anything might have happened to you.'

Michelle grinned and patted her pocket.

'I always carry a can of mace with me,' she said. 'For protection. Anyone tries anything, they'll get a faceful. This way, I level the playing field.'

As Michelle parked outside Jake's flat, Jake was

worrying about the book cover. His whole story depended on it. He hoped it was still in his flat. Or had the two men taken it? His kidnapping was definitely connected to the hidden books, of that he was sure. But who'd done it? And why?

But when they got into his flat, Jake was relieved to see the book cover was still where he'd left it, on the kitchen table.

'This is what it's about,' said Jake, picking it up and giving it to Michelle.

Michelle looked at the piece of ancient black leather, puzzled. She turned it over in her hands, examining it briefly, then put it back on the table and turned to Jake, her expression as puzzled as before.

'I don't understand,' she said. 'What is it? And what's that symbol on it?'

'That's the symbol of the Order of Malichea,' explained Jake. 'And that thing is the protective cover of a book that was hidden over five hundred years ago.'

Michelle looked at the piece of leather with new interest.

'Wow,' she said. Then she frowned. 'Why was it hidden?'

'OK,' said Jake. 'What I'm going to tell you is going to sound weird, but it's all true. And I can back it up.'

Michelle studied Jake warily.

'Is this going to be one of those "I was abducted by

aliens" things?' she asked. 'Because we get a lot of those, and my editor says they're a No-no.'

'No, it's nothing like that,' said Jake. 'It's very practical, but it is a government secret.'

Michelle still looked suspicious.

'We also get a lot of people coming to us with conspiracy stuff,' she said. 'You know, the government's using radio waves to control our minds. That sort of thing. This isn't one of those, is it?'

'No,' said Jake. 'It's about a secret scientific library that was hidden five hundred years ago, and why the government doesn't want it found.'

Michelle still didn't look convinced.

'This doesn't sound like a major-interest story,' she sighed. 'For one thing, five hundred years means it's all in the past.'

'No,' Jake corrected her. 'The books were hidden then. What's happening because of them is happening *now*.' He looked rueful. 'Me being kidnapped, for one thing.'

'Yes, but you being kidnapped and tied up for a couple of hours is nothing,' said Michelle. 'It doesn't look like there's anything *big*. No killings or sex scandals. No celebrities involved.'

'Oh, there have been killings,' said Jake, and he remembered the dead man in his living room, and Carl Parsons stabbed to death by Lauren.

Michelle hesitated, then she said: 'OK, you've got my interest, for the moment. Let's see if you can keep it going.' She looked around the kitchen. 'My guess is, this is going to take a bit of time. You got any coffee? Just in case I get bored and start to fall asleep.'

Jake couldn't help but grin at that. Michelle could only have been about the same age as him, yet she was acting as if she was a hard-bitten, tough old reporter who'd seen it all and was determined not to be impressed. But Jake remembered the look on her face when he'd first seen her, when she'd taken that blindfold off his eyes.

He put on the kettle to make coffee for them.

'What I know I got from a friend of mine,' he said. 'She's sort of an expert on it.'

'Maybe I should talk to her,' said Michelle.

'That would be difficult,' said Jake. 'She's in New Zealand. And there's a government ban on talking to her about any of this. If you tried, your system would be shut down, whether it's phone, email or Skype. Trust me, I've tried.'

'OK.' Michelle nodded. 'Now I'm more interested.'

'Right,' said Jake. 'A lot of the history stuff I'm going to tell you is available on the internet, but you'll need to know about it so you realise what's happening now.'

'Still interested,' said Michelle, 'but only if you get on with it.'

Jake nodded and began.

'The seventh and eighth centuries saw scholars from across the globe come to the monastery at Lindisfarne on Holy Island, off the north-east coast of Britain. It was the centre for all learning in the known world,' he told her. 'They exchanged ideas on a huge range of topics, especially the sciences. The library at Lindisfarne held most scientific knowledge of that time and an Order dedicated to the development of science sprang up there. This was the Order of Malichea.'

Michelle looked at the embossed symbol on the black leather cover on the kitchen table.

'These people?' she said.

Jake nodded.

'In 793, the Vikings invaded Britain. The monks of Lindisfarne were afraid that the Vikings would come to Holy Island, and if they did they'd destroy the library with all these precious scientific texts. So they reckon that some members of the Order of Malichea decided to take all the scientific texts away to a sympathetic monastery in northern France, where the library would be safe.

'The library of scientific texts, now held by the Order of Malichea at Caen in France, was added to, with scientists from all faiths, all nations, bringing their researches.'

'Yeah, and?' complained Michelle.

'And so the library of the Order of Malichea in the monastery in Caen became the hub of all knowledge of the global scientific community.

'But when the Inquisition spread beyond Spain to Italy, and there were real fears that the Inquisition would spread through the rest of Continental Europe —'

'This is the one where they burnt all the unbelievers and heretics.' Michelle nodded. 'I saw a documentary about it.'

'That's the one,' agreed Jake. 'The Order of Malichea in Caen were worried: lots of the scientific works in their library were by Arabic or Islamic scholars, and many dated from pre-Christian Roman or Greek times. For that reason alone, most of them would be considered heretical, and would be destroyed, as would any texts that went against the orthodox Church view of the world. Not to mention the monks would be burned as heretics. So they moved the library again.

'A party of monks was sent to Britain, under the guise of making a pilgrimage to Glastonbury. Each monk took with him a number of books. And at Glastonbury Abbey they hid the library in secret rooms behind the official library.'

'This is the same Glastonbury of King Arthur and the Holy Grail and all that?' asked Michelle.

Jake shook his head.

'It's the same Glastonbury,' he said, slightly irritated at her interruption, 'but it's nothing to do with King Arthur or the Holy Grail. This is about something real, not fictional.'

'There are plenty of people who think King Arthur was real,' pointed out Michelle. 'He's even mentioned in old history books of the time.' She smiled.

'Yes, well, this *isn't* about King Arthur,' stressed Jake.

'A pity,' said Michelle. 'If it was, that might be worth a story.'

'Can I get on with it?' asked Jake, an impatient edge to his tone.

Michelle nodded and sipped at her coffee. Jake continued.

'Even at Glastonbury the books weren't safe, because over the years the threat of the Inquisition spread, and the Church in Britain also began to seek out and destroy heretical thinking in its ranks. So, in 1497 the monks of the Order were told to take these so-called heretical science books and hide them in secure places, hiding each book in a separate place. To ensure the books would not be discovered, each book was to be hidden in a place that was unlikely to be disturbed because it was either sacred, or said to be cursed, or claimed to be haunted. A coded list of the different books and their hiding places was kept, known as The Index.

'Once the threat of the Inquisition had passed, and the books had been recovered they would be returned to the abbey library. However, the Inquisition didn't pass. The books stayed hidden.

'The Index, the supposed list of where the scientific books were hidden, would be a key piece of evidence these "lost sciences" existed. 'But no one knows what happened to it,' concluded Jake.

Michelle studied Jake over her coffee cup. She didn't look impressed.

'I still don't get it,' she said.

'You don't get what?' asked Jake.

'Why all this fuss over these old books. Yes, so they've been hidden. So what? Why should anyone be bothered about them, except historians and these geeks who go hunting for old things?'

'Because of the information they contain,' said Jake. 'Stuff like invisibility; turning ordinary metal into gold; the quest for eternal life; raising the dead . . .'

Michelle laughed.

'Oh, come on!' she said. 'This is just weird stuff! We're not talking real science here!'

'Yes we are,' insisted Jake. 'I saw it. Three months ago one of these books was dug up in a field in Bedfordshire. It contained details of how to create food from thin air, using fungal spores. And inside the book there were some of these spores, and some builder working at the site picked up the book and breathed in the spores, and turned into some sort of human vegetable. His whole body was covered in a fungus . . .'

Michelle shook her head.

'Urban legends,' she said. 'These sort of stories come up all the time. People turning into things. Werewolves . . .'

'I was there,' said Jake again. 'I saw it happen.'

Michelle looked at him curiously.

'How?'

'Because I'm a press officer with the Department of Science. I was sent to cover the story about a protest going on at this site where they were going to build a new university science block. I saw the book dug up. I saw the man pick it up. I saw him turn into this . . . thing.'

'Why wasn't there anything on the news about it?' challenged Michelle.

'Because my department slapped a D notice on the story, stopping it,' said Jake. 'But I know it happened. And I've seen the book. I held it in my hands.'

Michelle looked at the old leather book cover on the table.

'That's it?' she asked, suddenly worried.

'No,' said Jake. 'That book was taken back into protective custody by the government. It's been hidden away, and all knowledge of it has been denied.' He gestured at the piece of ancient black leather. 'This is from another one, and it's just the cover. Someone sent it to me.'

'Why?'

'I don't know. Either to rope me in, or as a warning to stay out of it. I don't know.'

Michelle fell silent, obviously thinking over everything Jake had said.

'Tell me again why these books are important *now*?' she asked.

'Because if anyone finds one with key information like that, they've got enormous power in their hands. And money. Say they find one with a cure for cancer. If they patent that information, they're rich for ever. Or say they'd got their hands on the one I saw dug up, the one where this dried fungus comes back to life and spreads as soon as it comes into contact with air.'

'Biological weapons,' muttered Michelle.

'Or a way of ending world hunger,' said Jake. 'Either way, it's power. And that is why so many people are after these books.'

'To make money.'

'Or, in the case of our government, and others, to stop the information coming out.' Jake sighed. 'They don't want our enemies having access to potential weapons like these.'

Michelle thought it over some more. Finally, she said: 'OK, I can see all that. But where's the story?'

Jake looked at her, astonished.

'That *is* the story,' he said. 'The hidden books. Powerful people after them. Others trying to stop them being found.' He appealed to her: 'This friend of mine said that if this library hadn't been hidden and the sciences had been tested, we'd have been on the moon five hundred years before we actually were. Plus treatments would have been found by now for most diseases. But the popes and kings of the time didn't want them known. The stuff in these books contradicted the official view of the world: that the Sun went round the Earth, and all that kind of stuff. They were seen as dangerous, so they were labelled heretical, or witchcraft or sorcery.'

Jake could see that Michelle was still weighing up what he'd told her. Finally she shook her head.

'It's still just a story,' she said. 'The sort you get in the weirdo tabloids: Elvis found on the moon. That sort of thing. Without hard evidence, there's no story.'

'I'm the hard evidence,' insisted Jake. 'What happened to me. First, I saw the book that was dug up, and what happened just now when you found me, tied up.'

Michelle shook her head again.

'That last could just be a prank. Everything else can be dismissed as hearsay. No, we need something concrete.'

Jake picked up the old cover.

'We've got this.'

'It's just a piece of old leather with some markings on it,' said Michelle. 'It's not evidence. No, we need one of these books. Something that can be tested and carbon-dated, and all those other things that scientists do these days.'

Jake hesitated, then he nodded.

'OK,' he said. 'I'll find one for you.'

It would be tough and he knew it. But if it meant he could bring Lauren back to England, he'd do it.

'I need to be there when you find it,' said Michelle. 'I want to see it uncovered. I don't want to be shown up as a sucker who fell for some scam with a fake.'

'Agreed,' said Jake.

'OK,' said Michelle. 'So where do we find one?'

'Well, that's not as easy as it sounds,' admitted Jake. 'Like I said, the books were hidden at a variety of places, all of them said to be sacred . . .'

'Cursed or haunted,' nodded Michelle. 'Yes, I got that. But you must have some idea where is most likely. Like Glastonbury, for example.'

Jake looked at her, curious.

'Glastonbury?' he said.

'Why not?' She shrugged. 'You said that was the last place they were kept. It's where they were taken from and hidden. No planes and trains and cars in those days. Sure, they could be spread all over the place, like the one that was dug up in . . . where?'

'Bedfordshire,' Jake reminded her.

'But I bet you a lot of them were hidden near Glastonbury.'

'You're still thinking about King Arthur, aren't you?' said Jake. 'Trying to fit him into your story.'

'Maybe,' admitted Michelle. 'But, you've got to admit, what I said about hiding them nearby makes sense.'

'Yes,' mused Jake thoughtfully. Then another thought struck him. 'And this Arthur business could work for us!'

'How?' asked Michelle.

'They're keeping an eye on me, and what I do.'

'Who?'

Jake sighed.

'Everybody. Certainly my own department, and MI5.'

Michelle looked at him suspiciously.

'MI5?' she queried. 'Where do they come in?'

'Like I said, in the wrong hands this information could be used to make the most dangerous weapons for terrorists. And they know I've been looking for the books. So if we put up a smokescreen, spread the word that at Glastonbury I'm just looking for stuff about King Arthur, nothing to do with the hidden books . . .'

42

'Do you think they'll believe that?' asked Michelle doubtfully.

'It's up to us to make them believe it,' said Jake. 'We make a few phone calls to each other about what we're going to be looking for at Glastonbury: Arthur and the Grail and stuff. They're bound to be listening in, they always do. If our cover's convincing enough, they'll come to that conclusion.'

'You hope,' said Michelle, still doubtful.

'It'll work,' said Jake confidently.

'OK.' Michelle nodded. 'When?'

'The sooner the better,' said Jake. 'Are you free this weekend?

'If this turns into a story, you bet. But you better not be wasting my time.'

'Don't worry, I'll dig out the list of possible sites where the books might have been buried, and sort out the most likely.'

'And I'll talk to my editor, see if he'll go for it.'

'You'd better not tell him about the hidden books at this stage,' cautioned Jake. 'If word gets out what we're up to, we might run into problems.'

'Don't worry, I'll push the King Arthur angle.' She smiled. 'I'm pretty sure he'll think it's a better story, anyway. More sellable. Do you have your own transport?'

'No,' said Jake. 'Public transport does for me.'

'OK, I'll pick you up on Saturday. Nine o'clock?'

'Great,' agreed Jake.

She headed for the door, a look of happy determination on her face. 'Glastonbury, here we come.'

Chapter 6

Once Michelle had gone, Jake started to see the flaws in the plan. It had all seemed so simple when he'd been talking to Michelle: go to Glastonbury, find a book, and put it in the public domain. But first: find a book. If it was that simple, then at least some of the books would have already been discovered by now; but there was nothing about them in Lauren's researches, or on the various internet sites about the Order of Malichea.

But that didn't mean they hadn't been dug up. He knew that Pierce Randall had already got at least one of the books, and his own Department of Science — or, rather, Gareth's secret service sub-section — had also got some of the books hidden away far from public gaze in the government archives. Or, perhaps, kept in some secret research establishments, where the sciences in the books were being tested.

Jake opened the box file where he kept Lauren's notes, and started to flick through them until he came to her 'List of possible hiding places'. He concentrated on those in the Glastonbury area, and soon had twelve named sites highlighted in yellow. He was just marking a thirteenth, when his phone rang.

'Jake Wells,' he said.

'Stop searching for the books.'

The voice was a man's, speaking low. It sounded as if it was muffled in some way, to stop it from being recognised.

'Excuse me?' said Jake, playing for time.

There was the briefest of pauses, then the voice said menacingly: 'Don't play games, Mr Wells. The Malichea books. Stop searching for them, or you will find yourself in serious trouble. *Very* serious trouble.'

'Is this a threat?' asked Jake, lightly, doing his best to sound casual.

'Yes it is,' said the voice, sounding even more menacing. 'You are being watched. If you don't stop looking for the books, you will be dealt with. People have died trying to find these books. You don't want yours to be the next death.'

Then all Jake could hear was the tone; the caller had hung up.

Immediately, Jake dialled 1471, but just got the time the call had been made, with the addition: 'The caller withheld their number.'

Yes, of course he did, thought Jake.

Who had it been? Gareth, possibly, or one of his minions. But why do this, when Gareth had already warned him off face to face?

The Watchers, possibly. The secret organisation dedicated to protecting the hidden books. But the Watchers didn't go in for violence. At least, not as far as he could make out. Not that this had been *actual* violence, just the threat of it. *You don't want yours to be the next death*. Very crude. But effective. Jake had already had experience of how ruthless the people in the whole Malichea business could be. This death threat may have just been a bluff, or it could be the real thing. But one thing Jake was sure: if finding one of the books could bring Lauren and he back together, then he'd take that chance.

He looked at his watch. It was just gone ten o'clock. In less than an hour he'd be talking to Lauren again, seeing her. Especially now he had A Plan. He switched on his computer and checked his emails, his heart lifting as he saw there was one from Lauren among all the usual spam.

He opened the email from Lauren, and felt a jolt of disappointment as he read it. *Hey Jake, Can't do Skype today/tonight because I've got to go into the office for a meeting. In fact, it looks as if I'm going to be in meetings every day this week, because there's a big Antarctic research expedition about to happen that we're involved in. And — with the twelve-hour time difference between us — the best time will be after I've finished work at the end of the week. I suggest this Friday at 8 p.m. (when it will be 8 o'clock on Saturday morning for you). Will that be OK? Or is that too early for you? We can make it later — 9 a.m. or 10 a.m.? Miss you lots, S xx.*

Although he felt the disappointment of not seeing Lauren that night, even though it was only on a computer screen, he still felt a sense of elation and excitement about what he was planning to do: go to Glastonbury and find one of the hidden books. OK, it was a bit of a wild shot, very chancy, but he wanted to tell her and share that hope with her, even though he knew that if he attempted to, their systems would shut down — email, phone call, Skype, whatever he used. It was so frustrating! If only he could find a way.

He clicked 'reply' and began to type:

'Hiya Sam, Skype this Friday/Saturday will be great — I love the fact that we can actually see one another, and know you're really there, and not just some figment of my imagination at the end of a keyboard.

Then a thought struck him. Maybe there was a way

round the bar on them. And this was a good time to test how far the censoring system worked. He added: *8 at night your time, 8 in the morning mine, will be great, as this Saturday I'm off to do some research into King Arthur and the Holy Grail.*

As he typed the words, he felt his chest tighten with nervous apprehension, waiting for his system to shut down . . . but it stayed connected. So far so good. Then, to test it further, he typed in, *At Glastonbury.*

His whole body tensed, waiting for the familiar 'click' and his screen to go blank . . . but the connection stayed up! It had worked! Obviously, Glastonbury was seen as 'safe' when it was linked to King Arthur and the Holy Grail. Computer says Yes.

He smiled to himself as he finished typing the rest of his message. *Love you, Jake xx*

Chapter 7

Jake left his small block of flats the next morning filled with a new sense of determination and purpose. He was going to Glastonbury. He would find one of the buried books. He'd bring Lauren back to England. He was just thinking these thoughts as the driver's door of the parked car he was passing jerked open, and a tall, tough-looking man in a dark suit got out of the car and stood directly in his path.

'Get into the car, please,' he said.

'What?' Jake said, bewildered.

Although the man was smartly dressed, there was no mistaking the air of menace about him. Military type, thought Jake hurriedly. Special forces.

'Into the car, please,' repeated the man, and he moved a step closer to Jake, his hands clenching and unclenching as if he was about to grab him. Jake stepped back, putting his hands up to defend himself, even though he knew this man could break him in half.

The rear door of the car swung open, nearly hitting Jake, and a cool calm voice said: 'That won't be necessary, Edward.' Then, in a friendly tone, the voice added: 'I'm here to offer you a lift to work, Jake.'

Jake peered into the back of the large expensive-looking car. Alex Munro, chief of the London office of Pierce Randall, beamed back at him.

'No thank you,' said Jake coldly. 'I think I'd rather take my chances on the buses.'

Munro sighed.

'Please, Jake. At the moment this is a genuine friendly gesture.'

Despite the smile on Munro's voice, and the lightness of tone, there was no mistaking the threat, in his 'at the moment'. Jake looked at the tall, hard-looking man, Edward, who was still standing mutely just within grabbing distance of Jake, poised to pounce if necessary.

'Come on, Jake,' said Munro. 'The buses are so unreliable and crowded these days.'

Jake hesitated, then climbed into the back of the car. Edward shut the rear door behind him, and then got into the front, behind the steering wheel. There was a glass partition between Jake and Munro, and Edward.

'Relax, Jake.' Munro smiled. 'I really am just going to give you a lift to your office.' He indicated a small cupboard set into the front of the luxurious rear compartment. 'Can I offer you anything? Tea? Coffee? Juice?'

Jake shook his head.

'No thank you,' he said coldly.

The car started up and moved off.

'So,' said Jake. 'What's so important that it brings the head of the most powerful law firm in Europe to my door?'

'The most powerful law firm in the *world*,' Munro corrected him.

And that was no exaggeration, reflected Jake. Pierce Randall had entered his life after he and Lauren had recovered one of the hidden books. Jake had never been sure how much of his troubles since had been because of Pierce Randall and the power they exerted.

On the surface, they were one of the most respectable and prestigious law firms ever, with branches all over the world. Their clients included most of the top companies and the most powerful governments. But there was another side to their operation, a darker side. Their client list also included international organised crime, as well as dictators and tyrants from some of the worst and most dangerous countries in the world. And, when secret deals were done between the respectable multinational companies and governments, and organised crime or a dubious tyrant, Pierce Randall would be the intermediary, making sure the deals were done with no fuss and no publicity, and the huge financial rewards allocated discreetly, with no trace.

Alex Munro was Head of Operations in Pierce Randall's London office, which was why Jake was stunned to see him out here, making this visit in person. When Jake had first met Munro, Munro had persuaded Jake that Pierce Randall wanted to find the hidden books of the Order of Malichea for altruistic purposes; to get the scientific information they contained out into the general arena, to help people, to use the new discoveries to save lives. Munro had been very plausible. It was only later that Jake had discovered the real reason that Pierce Randall wanted the hidden books: in two words, power and money. As Jake had told Michelle, if one of the books contained a cure for a previously untreatable terminal illness, whoever found that information and patented it would have a licence to print money. And the weapons potential of some of the sciences that were rumoured to be hidden would give dictators and terrorists power that was too hideous to consider.

Munro settled back into the luxurious leather seats and looked at Jake.

'You're suspicious of us, Jake, but you have no reason to be. We're after the same thing: the secret library.'

'But for different reasons,' said Jake. 'I want it to help the world. You want it to keep it hidden and make money from it.'

Munro sighed and smiled.

'You sound just like your friend, Ms Graham,' he said. 'How is she, by the way? I understand the government shipped her off somewhere, with a new identity. That must be very upsetting for you, to be parted from her in this way.'

He knows, thought Jake. He knows where Lauren is. Pierce Randall know everything. Except where the hidden books are.

Jake kept silent, just looked out through the darkened windows at the streets outside. Munro couldn't be trusted. Whatever he was here to offer was suspect. But why was he here?

As if reading Jake's thoughts, Munro said: 'We can help you get Ms Graham back.'

Jake swung round towards him, suspicious, but alert.

'She's in exile,' he said. 'The government say she can't return for ten years. Maybe more.'

Munro smiled.

'Ah, *governments*,' he said, with a sarcastic tone. 'Governments come and go. Government ministers change at an almost daily rate. We have . . . *friends* in high places. And, we are used to doing deals at the very top level, as I'm sure you are aware.'

'Why me?' asked Jake. 'You've got a big organisation. You can find them yourself. You've already got some of them.'

'Some,' admitted Munro. 'But you have something that our own operatives don't have, Jake. Passion. Desperation. We *want* to find these books. You *need* to find them, or at least one, to get your Ms Graham released from exile. Publicise it. Tell the world about it. Get the story about the Order of Malichea out into the open.'

He's been talking to Michelle, Jake realised, as he heard his own words to Michelle echoed back at him. And then he remembered that he hadn't told Michelle *why* he wanted to get the story about the books into the public domain, just that the story needed to be out there. So maybe Munro hadn't talked to Michelle after all. It was just Munro, keeping his finger firmly on the pulse of anything to do with Malichea.

'I'm sure that you will find a book. Maybe more than one. The deal I'm offering you is that you can keep one to do all the publicity you want, but we share it. You keep the actual book, we keep the rights to the information inside it.'

'To sell it,' said Jake.

'We already have clients ready to buy the appropriate technology.' Munro smiled. Again. 'And what is wrong with that? A book has a cure for illness, and a drug company puts that into practice and gets it out into the wide world. Millions of lives saved. Another book might have information about anti-gravity. An aerospace company uses that information to make safer planes. Again, millions of lives saved, the world becomes a better place.'

'Or one book contains previously undiscovered weapons technology and you sell it to a bunch of terrorists or criminals, who then use it to kill millions.'

Munro shrugged.

'We're talking morality,' he said. 'One person's lifesaver is another person's destruction. What I'm offering you is an opportunity to get back with your friend.'

Jake fell silent, weighing up Munro's offer. There was no doubt in his mind that Munro could fix it and get him reunited with Lauren. Maybe not necessarily in England, but that didn't matter to Jake. He didn't have any family to miss, no one he was close to, except Lauren. Anywhere in the world would do, as long as he and Lauren were together again. But it was a big price to pay, and he wasn't sure if Lauren would ever forgive him if she found out that he'd passed one of the books to Pierce Randall, and the science in it had been used for evil purposes.

'Well?' asked Munro.

Jake shook his head.

'No,' he said.

Munro sighed.

'You're making a big mistake, Jake,' he said. 'We'll get most of the books on our own, anyway. I'm offering you a great opportunity.'

'No,' said Jake again. 'You're using Lauren and me to help yourself and your clients.'

'Not all our clients are bad people,' countered Munro.

'The ones with the real money are,' said Jake.

Munro fell silent. His smile had gone.

'Very well,' he said. 'But, if you change your mind, you can always get hold of us.' And he took out a small business card and passed it to Jake. 'Remember, you owe us. We got you off that murder rap, gratis.'

'And there's no such thing as a free lunch,' said Jake bitterly.

Munro nodded.

'I believe that's what people say,' he said pleasantly.

Chapter 8

Exactly as Munro had promised, the car dropped Jake off outside the main entrance to the Department of Science. Jake waited until the car had pulled away, then he took out his phone and dialled the number Michelle had given him. His surprise meeting with Munro had given him even more determination to find a book and get it out into public knowledge as fast as he could. Michelle answered straight away.

'I've got the list of potential Arthur sites,' Jake told her. 'Can we meet today? I need to talk about them with you before the weekend.'

'OK, can you come to the office?' asked Michelle.

'No problem,' said Jake. 'Where is it?'

'Villiers Street, just off the Strand.'

'Fine,' said Jake.

He took the address of the *Qo* offices from her, and arranged to meet her at 12.30.

They met in the foyer of the building, and they walked down to the small public gardens by the Embankment. Jake gave Michelle the list of sites at Glastonbury he'd marked, while she unpacked her lunch from a plastic box.

'I've taken out all those that are on places that are too public, like the grounds of the abbey itself, or on National Trust land, or where buildings have been put up. All the others are on open land, most of them now farmland, and some of them parks that come under the local council.'

Michelle studied the list thoughtfully as she chewed her sandwich.

'The problem is: what might happen once we start digging,' said Jake. 'We start doing it on public land, the council could turn up and stop us. We do it on private land and we could get caught by the landowner.'

'That's not a problem,' said Michelle confidently. 'Ignore the council-owned lands and concentrate on those where the land is owned privately. Most land-owners are usually happy to let treasure hunters search their land for fifty per cent of the profit of whatever they find. Do you remember that Roman helmet they found in Cumbria recently?'

'No,' said Jake.

'The farmer and the treasure hunter split the prof-its fifty-fifty,' said Michelle. 'The helmet sold for two million. Trust me, any farmer will be happy to let you dig up his land if he thinks there might be that kind of money at the end of it.' She studied the list again. 'We need to find out who these bits of land belong to and get in touch with them. Tell them we're archaeologi-cal treasure hunters looking for stuff about King Arthur, and we'll share the proceeds of anything we find.' She frowned thoughtfully. 'The trouble will be finding out who owns what. We need planning info, and that can take time.'

Suddenly Jake thought of Robert, Lauren's cousin, the architect. He was always involved in planning issues.

'I think I may know someone who can get that infor-mation,' he said.

'Before the weekend?' queried Michelle.

'Yes,' said Jake.

He said this confidently, because he knew that Robert was almost as keen as he was to get Lauren back to England.

'Good,' said Michelle. She smiled. 'We have a plan.'

Jake waited until Michelle had left to go back to her office before he phoned Robert.

'Robert,' he said, 'it's Jake.'

'Jake! How are you?' boomed Robert's voice cheerfully in his ear. 'Long time no speak!'

'Yes, I'm sorry about that,' Jake apologised. 'I kept meaning to get in touch, but things seemed to keep turning up.'

'No problem!' said Robert. 'We're talking now.'

'Yes,' agreed Jake. 'Actually, Robert, I wondered if we could meet up.'

Something in Jake's tone must have alerted Robert that this wasn't just a social call, because he hesitated before replying: 'Yes, of course.' Although his voice was just as cheerful as before, Jake could hear a note of caution in it, but knew that luckily Robert was smart enough not to blurt out anything over the phone. They'd already learnt that it was very easy for people to bug their phone conversations.

'How about after work today?' suggested Jake.

'Excellent!' said Robert. 'You know the Pret a Manger in Oxford Street, the one at the Tottenham Court Road end?'

'Yes,' said Jake.

'Half past five?'

'Great,' said Jake. 'I'll see you then.'

As he hung up, he thought: clever Robert. He'd worked out that whatever Jake wanted to talk to him about concerned Lauren, and they wouldn't want their conversation overheard. So he'd chosen a nice but obvious location, a fairly noisy café, where any opposition would get there first to eavesdrop on them. And, once they'd met up, Jake and Robert would head elsewhere, to a place it would be difficult to have their conversation listened to. Not impossible — Jake had already discovered that conversations could be listened to any place anywhere, such was the power of modern surveillance technology. But at least he and Robert would make it difficult for any listeners.

Robert was waiting at Pret a Manger when Jake arrived.

'Coffees?' asked Jake.

'Later,' said Robert. 'There's this fabulous jazz CD I want to get first. We can grab a coffee afterwards.'

Jake followed Robert out of the coffee bar and they headed westwards along Oxford Street.

'HMV,' announced Robert. 'We'll try there first. If they haven't got it, there's a specialist shop I know in Soho we can try.'

As they walked, they talked, just like two old friends catching up. Which, of course, they were, but in this case their mutual point of contact was Lauren, and the hidden library of Malichea. Like Jake, Robert had been in contact with Lauren in New Zealand, Skyping and emailing.

'She seems to be settling in there all right,' he said.

'Yes,' agreed Jake, not wholly enthusiastically.

'She misses you, though,' said Robert.

'Does she?' said Jake, cheering up.

'It's a pity you can't go over there and see her,' said Robert.

Jake sighed.

'The powers-that-be are determined that she and I will never be in the same country again,' he said gloomily. 'Not even on the same continent.' Then he added in a whisper: 'But I've got a plan to change that.'

'I thought you might have,' said Robert. 'What is it?'

'I'm going to find one of the books and go public with it. Once I've done that they won't be able to keep the Order of Malichea secret, and they'll let Lauren come back.'

Robert didn't look convinced.

'Are you sure of that?' he asked doubtfully.

'Pretty sure.' Jake nodded. 'After all, why are they keeping her in New Zealand? To stop her finding any of the books and letting the world know about them. So I'm going to do it for her.'

Robert thought it over as they walked, and finally he asked: 'How?'

'I've got a journalist on board who says she'll run the story if we can find one of the books. And I've got a pretty strong idea I know where's the best place to find one.'

'Where?'

'Glastonbury,' said Jake.

Robert shook his head.

'They'll stop you,' he said. 'That character, Gareth Whateverhisname is.'

'Findlay-Weston,' said Jake. 'And no he won't, because I'm going to pretend to be looking for stuff about King Arthur and the Holy Grail.'

Robert still didn't look convinced.

'He won't believe you,' he said.

'It's worked so far,' said Jake, and he told Robert how the connection didn't go down when he mentioned King Arthur.

Robert frowned as he thought it over. By now they'd reached HMV, and Jake followed Robert into the store. The place was as crowded as ever, which Jake hoped would make the job of anybody listening to them harder.

'It *might* work,' Robert said, still doubtful.

'Have you got a better idea how to get her back?' asked Jake.

'No,' admitted Robert. 'So, you want me to come and help you find this book?'

'Actually, I wanted your help about getting permission to dig for it,' said Jake. 'You know, who owns which bit of land, that sort of thing. So we can contact the landowners and get permission.'

Jake looked around to make sure no one was paying too much attention to them, then passed Robert the short list with the names of the possible sites he'd selected. Robert studied the list.

'Four of them,' he said. 'All farms.'

'That's right,' said Jake.

'When are you planning to go?' he asked.

'The sooner the better,' said Jake. 'This weekend. Spend the first day searching around, and some serious digging on the Sunday.'

Robert shook his head again.

'You're mad,' he said. He tapped the list. 'Some of these places will have hundreds of acres of ground, maybe thousands. You could dig for a year and not find anything.'

'That's why I was going to spend the first day checking the places out.'

'And look for what — a big cross and a sign saying '"Dig here for ye ancient book"?' commented Robert sarcastically.

Jake looked uncomfortable.

'All right, it's a big task, I'll give you that,' he admitted. 'But have you got anything better?'

Robert grinned and stuffed the list into his inside pocket.

'I certainly have,' he said. 'A sniffer dog.'

Jake looked at Robert, baffled.

'A what?' he asked.

'A sniffer dog,' repeated Robert. 'One of the guys I play rugby with, Andy Beamish, is part of a search and rescue team, and he uses a sniffer dog to find things like people trapped under rubble, dead bodies, explosives and drugs, even pirate CDs. These dogs are amazing!' Then his face clouded. 'The trouble is, we'd need something with the scent for the dog to find.' He let out a heavy sigh. 'A pity you never kept the packet that last book was in. That would have been ideal! The smell of the oilskin, or whatever it was wrapped in.'

'But I've got one!' burst out Jake excitedly. Then he stopped himself and looked quickly around, but no one in the store seemed to react to his sudden outburst. He leant forward. 'I've got one,' he repeated excitedly, but this time in a whisper.

'Where from?' asked Robert, puzzled.

Jake told him about the ancient cover mysteriously appearing on his kitchen table.

'And you've got no idea who put it there?' asked Robert.

'No,' said Jake. He grinned. 'But the main thing is, I've got it! And we can use it for this dog!'

'Excellent,' said Robert. 'Right, I'll get in touch with Andy and see if he's free this weekend. I did have something arranged for Saturday, but I can change that.'

Jake frowned.

'I didn't expect you to come as well,' he said. 'Not after what happened last time, nearly getting yourself killed.'

Robert fixed Jake with a firm glare.

'Are you expecting to get attacked again?' he demanded.

'Well . . . no,' said Jake. 'I hope not.'

'Well, even if you were, you wouldn't keep me away from this,' Robert told him firmly. 'Like you say, this could get Lauren back to England. And if so, I want to be part of it.' He tapped his inside pocket where he'd put the list of places. 'Right, I'd better start checking who the landowners are, and get on to them and get their permission to start digging.' He grinned. 'This could be brilliant!'

Chapter 9

After he left Robert, Jake phoned Michelle.

'Good news,' he told her. 'The friend I was telling you about says he'll sort out the digging permission for us. And also, he's going to fix up a sniffer dog.'

'A what?' asked Michelle, puzzled.

'A sniffer dog,' repeated Jake. 'He says the area we're looking for is too large for us to have a chance with random digging, and if we're serious about finding anything from King Arthur's time, a sniffer dog will be just the thing we need.'

'Excellent!' said Michelle. 'I'll bring a camera. If we find anything it'll go a long way to backing up our story.'

'Good idea,' said Jake.

'Oh, by the way, a change of plan,' said Michelle. 'Has your friend got transport?'

Jake thought of Robert's noisy old van.

'Yes,' he said. 'Why?'

'I was thinking of popping in on some old friends of mine on the way there,' she said. 'I haven't seen them in ages. They're in Salisbury, so I thought I'd see them on Friday and stay the night, and then go on to Glastonbury from there. I'd invite you, but you don't know them, and it'll be boring for you, old friends catching up. I wouldn't have mentioned it if you hadn't said about your friend coming as well. If he can take you, that would be great.'

'That's fine by me,' said Jake. 'We'll meet at Glastonbury on Saturday.'

'I've booked us in at the Grail and Thorn,' she said. 'The booking's under my name, Faure, if you get there first.'

Jake was slightly taken aback at this.

'But . . .' he began.

'Listen, Glastonbury gets booked up with all these Arthur pilgrims every weekend,' said Michelle. 'You've got to move quickly if you want to get a room.'

A room? One? Warning bells sounded in Jake's head.

'Actually . . .' he began awkwardly.

'Don't worry about the cost,' she said. 'My editor said it sounds like a good story, so the magazine is picking up the tab.

'When you say "get a room" . . .' he said.

'Rooms,' she corrected him quickly. 'Two.'

'Oh,' said Jake, relieved.

'Let's get something clear, Jake,' she said, and now there was a new note in her voice: a warning tone: 'I don't know if you were thinking that we might be sharing a room . . .'

'No no!' said Jake quickly.

'But that's not what this is about,' continued Michelle.

'No, of course not,' said Jake awkwardly.

God, he felt such an idiot.

'Good,' she said. 'I'll see you at Glastonbury on Saturday.'

Jake arrived home, feeling invigorated. Robert's suggestion of using a sniffer dog was a stroke of brilliance. If there was a book to be found, using the dog they'd find it, Jake was sure. In a matter of just a couple of days, ever since he'd come home to find that old book cover on his kitchen table, he'd found a whole new confidence in what he was doing. He'd have Lauren back, and sooner than either of them had expected, of that he was certain!

He walked into his kitchen, glancing at the table, half expecting to find another book cover left on it — perhaps this time a whole book! But the table was clear.

He turned towards the kettle to make himself a drink, and as he did so, he saw the picture. It was stuck to the wall with a knife. It was a photo of Lauren, and her face had a red cross slashed over it, like blood. Underneath the photo were scrawled the words: *Samantha Adams*, followed by her address in New Zealand. And then the warning: *Don't go to Glastonbury*.

Chapter 10

Jake's mind was in turmoil. They knew who Lauren was. They knew her so-called secret identity. They knew where she lived in New Zealand. And they knew that Jake was planning to go to Glastonbury.

Who were they?

He tried to think of who knew about Lauren becoming Samantha Adams in Wellington. Gareth, obviously. And he was fairly sure that Pierce Randall knew the secret, they seemed to know everything. But Pierce Randall had wanted Jake to find the books for them, not for them to remain hidden. The only people he knew who wanted the books to stay secret were the Watchers, and Gareth and the government people he worked for. Everyone else was after the books because of what they offered: power and money. Was this threat from some organisation that wanted to stop Jake from interfering with their own search for the books? Was it the same people who'd phoned him and threatened him? And now, they were threatening Lauren.

He had to warn her. But how, without the automatic censors cutting them off? If he could Skype her or phone her, he might just be able to get a warning out before the system shut down.

He looked at the clock. Eight o' clock. It would be eight in the morning in Wellington.

He picked up his phone and dialled her home number. It rang, and continued ringing. As he hung up, he reflected that she must have gone into the office to make sure she was there for these meetings she'd mentioned, the forthcoming Antarctic expedition. At least, he hoped that was why she wasn't answering.

He tried her mobile number, but all he got was the voicemail asking him to leave a message.

Surely they wouldn't have done anything to her yet?

His fingers trembled as he switched on his computer and went to his emails, and then relaxed slightly as he read one from Lauren.

Jake. If you try and call, I've had to go to the office early for a meeting about the Antarctic expedition.

Just as I thought, mused Jake.

As it's for a meeting, all phones will be off. But I'll talk to you on Friday (Saturday your time) as we said. So, King Arthur! Wow! Sounds really interesting. Wish I was with you! Who are you going with? Or will this trip be on your own? Got to go. Love you lots, S. xxx

Jake sat and read the message again. She was all right. At least, she *seemed* to be OK. He started to type a reply, then he stopped. Should he tell her he was going with Robert *and* Michelle? Then he'd have to explain who Michelle was. A reporter. A young woman reporter, and Lauren might get the wrong idea of what was going on.

He felt sure Lauren knew she could trust him, but, this far apart, with no way of talking things through and explaining things face to face . . .

He typed: *I'm going with Robert and a rugby pal of his.*

For once, he was glad they weren't on Skype. If he'd tried saying that on camera to her, she'd see through him straight away and know he wasn't telling her the whole story. And then, when she discovered about Michelle, she'd wonder why.

I'll tell her about Michelle later, he determined. After we've got the book. I'll tell her I didn't want to say anything about her in case the opposition picked up on it and realised we were really after one of the hidden books.

It was a lame excuse, and he felt guilty because he knew he was lying to Lauren, but he didn't want her thinking he might be interested in anyone else while she was away.

He typed some more, innocuous chatter about how

good it had been to see Robert again, and things that were happening in Britain, and then added the heartfelt core of his message: *Be careful. There could be some nasty people over there. Someone here seems to know who and where you are. I don't want anything to happen to you. I miss you. Jake. xx*

When he'd sent it, he went on to the internet. If he was going to Glastonbury under the pretence of looking for Athurian artefacts, then it would be a good idea to do some research on the subject, just in case anyone started asking him questions. He typed in 'King Arthur', and almost immediately thousands of websites were listed. He went through them methodically, particularly those where there was a link to Glastonbury. It took a couple of hours, but it was time he felt was worth it. For one thing, if Gareth's spooky minions were monitoring his computer activity, this would go a long way to convincing them that he really was interested in King Arthur and the Grail legends.

The legends surrounding Glastonbury seemed to begin with stories of Jesus Christ coming to Britain. One said that he was brought to Britain as a child by his uncle, a wealthy trader called Joseph of Arimathea, and that they ended up at what was to become the site of Glastonbury Abbey. Another said that after Jesus had been crucified and resurrected, Joseph of Arimathea came to this site at a place called Wearyall Hill, and stuck his traveller's staff into the ground. That staff blossomed and became the Glastonbury Thorn, a bush that still flowered twice a year — once at Christmas and once at Easter.

Joseph built a simple church at the site. He was also said to have brought the Holy Grail with him to Britain, the cup used by Jesus at the last supper, and in which it was said that Joseph caught some of Christ's blood while he was on the cross at Calvary.

As if this wasn't legend enough, it was also believed that King Arthur had been buried at the site when it was still an island called Avalon. According to another website, during the reign of Henry II, the monks of the abbey unearthed a tomb and a lead cross, on which was carved, in Latin: *Here lies the famous King Arthur, buried in the Isle of Avalon*. The body found in the tomb was then reburied in the abbey itself.

'Wow,' Jake murmured to himself. 'No wonder the place attracts so many myth hunters!' As well as numerous references to King Arthur of legend, and his Knights of the Round Table, Jake found one reference from an ancient history book, written about AD 600, which talked of 'Arthur, King of the Britons, leading his troops against the invaders and defeating them at the Battle of Badon Hill'.

Another search indicated that 'Badon Hill' was not far from Bath.

'Which puts it all in the same area as Glastonbury,' mused Jake. He smiled to himself. This was looking good. This would be just the sort of stuff he'd be unearthing if he really *was* planning to look for relics of Arthur. And maybe even the Holy Grail itself. He hoped that whoever was watching him was monitoring his computer activity. His cover story was looking good.

Chapter 11

8 a.m. Saturday, and Jake was smiling into his webcam and looking at Lauren on his computer screen. His overwhelming feeling was relief that she looked OK, safe and well. But the expression on her face showed something was worrying her.

'That email of yours . . .' she began.

'Careful,' warned Jake quickly. 'We don't want to get cut off before we start to talk.'

Lauren hesitated, then nodded, but asked: 'These people you mentioned . . .'

'I don't know who they are,' said Jake quickly. 'I just got an anonymous message. I just wanted to let you know so you'd take care, just in case.'

Just in case they come after you, Jake meant. He wondered how much he could say without the censor cutting them off. He decided to change the topic to something lighter, and then maybe he could slip in a clearer warning later.

'So, King Arthur,' he said jovially. 'What do you think?'

'You and Robert looking for the Holy Grail.' Lauren smiled. 'Just like two knights of old.'

'Why not?' said Jake lightly. 'Sir Jake and Sir Robert. Anyway, I thought it was time I took up a new interest. Something a little less . . . problematic.'

This was for the sake of whoever might be listening in, just to assure them that the trip he was planning to Glastonbury was harmless. He didn't know if it would work, but it was worth a try. At least they hadn't been cut off.

'What about you?' he asked, changing the subject. 'The Antarctic expedition?'

It was obviously a topic that Lauren was delighted to talk about, because Jake listened happily for the next ten minutes as Lauren outlined the forthcoming expedition. 'And they say I might even get a chance to go on one!' she ended excitedly.

'Wow!' said Jake, impressed and jealous at the same time. 'I wish I could go with you.'

Lauren smiled.

'Who knows,' she said. 'Maybe one day we can.'

The sound of Jake's mobile ringing interrupted them. Jake picked it up, and looked at the screen.

'It's Robert,' he announced. Then he put the phone down. 'I'll call him back.'

'You'd better talk to him,' said Lauren. 'It's obviously about your boys' weekend.'

Jake hesitated momentarily, then nodded. His phone had stopped ringing, but Jake knew Lauren was right. They needed to get to Glastonbury and find the book, get the evidence that would bring Lauren back.

'OK,' he said. 'I'll let you know how we get on.'

'Give Robert my love,' said Lauren. 'And this kiss is for you.'

And she blew him a kiss.

'I'll be thinking of you,' Jake told her.

'I'll be thinking of you,' she said back.

Then they disconnected.

Immediately, Jake dialled Robert's number.

'Hi, Robert,' he said. 'You called. All ready for the trip?'

'No I am not!' snarled Robert.

He was angry. No, he was more than angry, he was absolutely furious.

'Do you know what those swines have done!' he bellowed. 'They've attacked Lizzie!'

For one horrible moment, Jake thought that Robert's fiancée had been attacked. Then he remembered her name was Gemma. He also just managed to recall in time that Lizzie was the name Robert gave to his van.

'What?!' he said, shocked. 'How?'

'They've slashed all her tyres, and they've put sugar in her petrol tank. So the old girl's not going anywhere!'

Chapter 12

They were an hour later than planned in setting off for
Glastonbury. Robert had hired a car for the weekend,
telling Jake determinedly when he'd pulled up outside
Jake's flat: 'If they think they can stop me, they've got
another thing coming!'

Robert's anger and his desire for revenge for the
attack on his beloved old van occupied the first half-
hour of the journey. For Jake, the big question was:
who had done it?

'Could it have been the Watchers?' he asked.

'But I thought you said they weren't violent types,'
Robert said.

'Well, not as far as I know.' Then Jake remembered
Carl Parsons, a Watcher, and secretly very violent. But
Parsons had been a renegade, a mercenary, so maybe
he didn't really count as a Watcher at all.

'Anyway, doing it to a van isn't the same as doing it

to a person,' said Jake, trying to make himself feel less threatened if it had been the Watchers.

'It feels the same,' said Robert angrily. 'I love my old van. And if it was them, and I catch hold of them, they're going to find out what physical violence really is!'

'We'd better tell the others about the Watchers,' said Jake. 'Your pal, Andy, and this reporter. So they know what we're up against.' He fell into a thoughtful silence, then added: 'Of course, it needn't have been the Watchers. It could have been someone trying to stop the competition.'

'We're supposed to be looking for King Arthur,' pointed out Robert.

'Yes, but the opposition may not believe our cover story,' put in Jake.

'I think we'll find out soon enough who it is,' grunted Robert. 'I bet you they'll be watching for us in Glastonbury.'

Which wasn't a pleasant prospect, Jake reflected.

'So what's this reporter like?' asked Robert.

'She's young, about the same age as me,' said Jake. 'Very ambitious, which is why I thought she'd be ideal. And also, she doesn't scare easily.' He told him about Michelle coming to look for him in the timber store. 'Plenty of people would have ignored it. Or maybe phoned the police and reported it.'

'But she didn't,' mused Robert. 'Suspicious?'

Jake thought it over.

'Yes and no,' he said. 'Yes, her getting the phone call. But no, because — like I say — she's ambitious, and if she thinks there's a chance to further her career, she'll go for it. Even if it could be a bit . . .'

'Dangerous?' queried Robert.

'I was going to say "chancy",' said Jake. 'But it could have been dangerous. So, yes.'

'She sounds interesting,' said Robert. 'I look forward to meeting her.'

As they drove, Jake couldn't help turning round every so often to check on the cars behind them.

'Why do you keep turning round?' asked Robert irritably, after Jake had twisted round in his seat for the fourth time.

'Seeing if anyone's following us,' replied Jake.

'They don't need to,' said Robert. 'Anyone who's been keeping tabs on us already knows we're going to Glastonbury. It makes more sense for them to be waiting for us there.'

Which was true, Jake had to admit.

The journey was uneventful, and it was midday when they finally pulled into the car park of the Grail and Thorn. After they'd checked in, Robert got hold of his pal, Andy, on his mobile, and Jake did the same with

Michelle. Both reported that they weren't far away from Glastonbury, and they agreed to meet up at the pub at one o'clock for lunch, and to draw up their plan of action.

Robert decided he wanted to go and freshen up after the journey, but Jake was keen to check out the town and get as much information as he could from the tourist office and the local shops. That way, he reasoned, it would help convince anyone who might be watching him that he really was in Glastonbury to find out about King Arthur and the Grail, and not searching for the hidden books. As he walked away from the Grail and Thorn, he couldn't help casting a sweeping look around to see if he could spot anyone who might be watching him. The trouble was, how would he know? Anyone who was keeping him under observation, and was good at their job, would be doing it without Jake being able to tell.

He tried committing the faces of some people to memory, choosing those he thought *looked* suspicious; but then he gave up. In a town like Glastonbury, that seemed to attract all sorts of oddballs, nearly everyone he saw could have been described as suspicious.

The town itself seemed to be aiming at two separate sorts of tourists: religious pilgrims, and ageing hippies. There were shops and information booths dedicated to the Christian history of Glastonbury: Joseph of Arimathea, the Holy Grail, St Dunstan, and the history of the abbey; but there were far more stores selling souvenirs of King Arthur and the Knights of the Round Table; and even more whose windows were crammed with crystals for divination, candles of all shapes and colours, magic pebbles and rocks, maps showing ley lines, and clothes that wouldn't have looked out of place in the 1960s.

Jake picked up three maps, one showing the tourist attractions in the town; another, a plan of the abbey, and the third a map showing Glastonbury Tor and the key places on it. He also bought a couple of slim books about the King Arthur and the Grail legend. By the time he got back to the pub, Michelle had arrived, and was sitting with Robert in the garden. With them at the table was a cheerful-looking guy with a large black and white dog.

'Jake, meet my rugby pal, Andy,' said Robert.

Jake and Andy shook hands.

'And the other one is his working partner, Woody, the wonder-dog,' put in Michelle.

Jake forced himself to give the dog a friendly smile. Jake had always been a bit wary of dogs. When Robert had first mentioned using a sniffer dog, he'd consoled himself with the thought that a sniffer dog would be trained and ought to be safe.

Andy rubbed the dog's head, and Woody's tail wagged heartily. He seems friendly enough, thought Jake. And, if it was true that dogs grew to be like their masters, then Andy certainly seemed a cheerful and open guy. He was shorter than Robert, but chunkily built, as fitted a rugby player. His hair was cropped short, possibly so that opposing players couldn't grab it in the scrum, reflected Jake. But then he remembered that Andy worked in search and rescue, so it was possibly a military thing.

'So, Robert says we're looking for some kind of book,' said Andy.

'Yes.' Jake sat down at their table.

'Valuable?'

'Yes and no,' said Jake. 'To be honest, it's only really worth anything to people who are interested in history.'

'History can be worth money,' said Andy.

'That's what I told Jake,' put in Michelle. 'That Roman helmet that's worth two million, for example.'

'Yes, well, this is nothing like that,' said Jake. He looked around, and then said in a low voice: 'Anyway, officially, that's not why we're here. We're looking for something of King Arthur. The Holy Grail, or something similar.' And he shot an accusing look at Robert.

'I had to tell Andy what we were looking for,' hissed back Robert defensively. 'After all, he and Woody are the ones who'll be searching for it. They had to know.'

'True,' admitted Jake reluctantly. But he wasn't happy about it. The more people who knew the real purpose of their visit to Glastonbury, the more chance there was of the opposition homing in on them. He looked at Andy as the search and rescue man rubbed the dog's ears, and the dog looked up at him, tongue lolling out of the side of his mouth, big brown eyes watching him.

'What breed is he?' he asked.

'Woody's a bitza,' said Andy. 'Bitza this, bits of that. There's a bit of collie in him, and a bit of setter, and I'm pretty sure there might even be a bit of blood-hound in him, because he's got such a fantastic nose! He can sniff out anything!'

'Yes, explosives and drugs and things like that. Robert told me,' said Jake. 'But aren't criminals able to get round it? I read somewhere that drug smugglers hide the drugs in crates packed with strong-smelling stuff like coffee to beat the dogs.'

Andy grinned.

'That depends on the quality of the dog. A woman in Australia was visiting her boyfriend in prison and she tried to smuggle in drugs in her bra. She tried to fool the detection dog by smearing her bra with coffee, pepper, and even Vicks VapoRub. The dog still smelt out the drugs.'

Michelle's face showed her disgust.

'God, her bra must have stunk enough for people to get suspicious, anyway.'

Andy continued, warming to describing the almost paranormal virtues of sniffer dogs. 'A sniffer dog can detect blood, even after it's been scrubbed off. Dogs smell things in parts per trillion, something way beyond the range of human beings. They can smell illnesses such as diabetes and cancers in a person.' He looked affectionately at Woody. 'From what Robert tells me, this thing you've got will be meat and drink to Woody, if it's as old as he says it is. The smells on it will be easily identifiable.'

Jake looked round carefully to make sure that no one seemed to be taking too much of an interest in them, then took the envelope from his pocket and passed it to Andy.

'This is what we're looking for,' he said.

Andy lifted the ancient blackened leather cover from inside the envelope, and smiled.

'Easy!' he said, pushing the book cover back inside the envelope and returning it to Jake. He turned to Robert. 'You said you knew some places where you thought this book might be buried?'

Robert nodded.

'Four of them,' he said. 'They're all out of town, on farmland. I've got permission from the landowners to search them.'

'Great!' said Andy. 'Well, the sooner we get started, the better.'

'Excellent.' Michelle nodded. She stood up. 'I'll get my camera.'

'First, lunch!' said Robert firmly. 'You people may be able to go all day without food, but I need my sustenance.'

Michelle looked as if she was about to argue, but one look at the determined and hungry expression on Robert's face and she shrugged.

'OK,' she said. 'Lunch it is.'

They ordered snacks, and while they ate, Jake took the opportunity to fill Michelle and Andy in on potential hazards.

'If we're lucky enough to find one of the books, whatever happens, don't open it,' he told them.

'Why not?' asked Andy.

Briefly, Jake told him what had happened when the book had been dug up accidentally in Bedfordshire.

'When the digger driver opened it, he released the fungal spores that were in the pages. As soon as they came into contact with moisture, which was his sweat, the spores turned into this heaving mass of fungus which covered him from head to toe.'

'Wow!' said Andy, impressed. 'What happened to him? Did they get the stuff off him?'

'I don't know,' admitted Jake. 'He was being kept in an isolation ward, but he was still covered in the

90

fungus.' He shrugged unhappily. 'I don't know whether he lived or died. I'm just telling you this so you know how dangerous these things can be. If we're lucky enough to find a book, we open it in strict safety conditions: hazard suits in a laboratory.'

'Great!' Michelle beamed. 'Pictures like that will make this story even better!'

'You also said you were going to tell them about the Watchers,' Robert reminded Jake.

'Yes.' Jake nodded.

Michelle frowned.

'The Watchers?' she asked.

'The Watchers are the guardians of the books,' said Jake. 'Originally, they were ordinary people who were trusted by the monks who hid the books. You know, cooks, servants, carpenters, stonemasons, tradespeople. The sort no one notices. Their job was to keep watch over the hidden books and make sure no one discovered them by accident, or on purpose. No one except the monks who'd hidden them, that is.'

'Sort of security?' asked Andy.

Jake nodded.

'Apparently, the idea was that the Watchers would keep the books safe until the time was right for them to be revealed. But that time never came. So the Watchers continued keeping watch over the books, making sure they remained undisturbed. The books are still hidden, and the Watchers still guard them. The job was handed down from generation to generation. Parents to their children. Uncles and aunts to nieces and nephews. They're still ordinary people doing ordinary jobs — only now they're nurses, teachers, railway workers, taxi drivers, carpenters, journalists . . .'

Andy frowned.

'Are you expecting trouble from these Watchers if we find anything?' he said, concerned.

'Not trouble as in physical violence,' said Jake. 'At least, the Watcher I met before told me they don't go in for that sort of thing.'

'What sort of things do they go in for?' asked Michelle.

'Interrupting any digging,' said Jake. 'Court orders. But all non-violent.'

'Well, at least that's something positive,' said Michelle.

Jake hesitated, wondering whether to tell them about Carl Parsons, the Watcher that Lauren had killed, and how he'd attacked her with a knife to try and force her to give him the book she and Jake had got hold of. But that had been because he was getting paid to get hold of the book, not because he was a Watcher.

'Mind,' he added, 'that's how *most* Watchers go about it. If there was a renegade among them . . .'

'He or she might get violent?' asked Andy.

Jake shrugged.

'It's unlikely,' he said. 'But I just thought I'd mention it.'

And let's hope that's true, he said silently to himself. The last thing they wanted was to come up against another Carl Parsons, armed and murderous.

Chapter 13

They drove out to the first site, Jake and Michelle with Robert in the hired car, and Andy with Woody in Andy's car. As Robert drove, Jake kept his attention on the other traffic around them, slotting into his memory any vehicles that looked as if they might be following them. The first site was a field down a narrow country lane, with barely room to park one car, let alone two.

'If anyone's following us, they're going to have to wait for us back at the road,' Jake commented.

'The only car that looked like it was coming after us was that blue Renault,' said Michelle, taking a trowel from the boot of the car. 'But it sailed straight past when we turned off down the lane.'

'It's still worth remembering,' put in Robert. 'If we see it again when we try the second site, we'll know they're definitely following us. Did anyone get the number?'

'I did,' Michelle said, and she read out the registration plate.

'Impressive,' said Jake approvingly.

Michelle shrugged.

'It's all part of being an investigative reporter,' she said, 'keeping my eyes open and my memory sharp.'

Andy joined them with Woody on the lead, obviously keen to get into action.

'All ready?' he asked.

Jake produced the envelope with the old book cover and passed it to Andy, who held the cover under the dog's nose for it to get a good scent, before returning it to Jake.

'OK,' said Andy. 'Let's go.'

They crossed a stile into the field Lauren had targeted, Woody and Andy leading the way, Michelle following with the trowel, then Jake and Robert bringing up the rear, each carrying a spade.

They walked along the side of the field, along a narrow earth-trodden path partly covered by nettles and long grass, with brambles snaking through that caught at their ankles as they walked. Jake's concentration was on Woody as the dog ambled along, nose sniffing at the ground. He was waiting for the dog to stop and show some interest, or excitement, but Woody's mood didn't change. He just sniffed all the way along the path to the end, and then along the path to the right that cut across the end of the field. At one point he stopped, and Jake's heart gave a little leap of hope, but the dog had only stopped to take a pee, and then they continued on again.

They arrived back at the point where they'd begun, having walked completely around all four sides of the large field, and Woody hadn't registered any reaction, apart from being interested in some of the different natural smells he came across.

'There's nothing here,' announced Andy.

'Maybe it's in the middle of the field?' suggested Jake hopefully, pointing to where the crops were growing.

'I promised the farmers we'd stick to the perimeters of the fields,' said Robert.

'Well, that's a bit ridiculous!' snapped Jake. 'Say it's out there in the field itself?'

'Then it's likely it would have been dug up years ago by a plough or a digger,' said Robert. 'Also, if I hadn't given them that undertaking, they wouldn't have let us on to their land. They don't want people walking across their fields ruining their crops.'

'Maybe the next field won't have anything growing in it,' said Michelle.

'Maybe,' agreed Robert. 'Let's go and find out.'

As they crossed the stile and headed back to the cars, Jake felt hollow. All right, it was asking a bit much for them to strike lucky the first time, but this *was* Glastonbury. If the books were going to be hidden anywhere, there was more chance of finding one here. And Lauren had listed this field as a likely spot.

They drove out of the country lane and on to the road, Jake keeping his eyes open for any sign of the blue Renault Michelle had spotted, but there was no sign of it. In fact, there was no sign of any cars following them during their trip to the lay-by near a path that led to the second field Lauren had listed.

This site was as empty as the first. This field had no crops growing, so they were able to ramble across the whole of it, but despite Woody covering every square metre of ground with his nose pressed to the short grass, he never gave any indication that there was anything to be found.

'Maybe they've been buried too deep,' suggested Michelle.

Andy shook his head.

'Trust me, if it was here, Woody would smell it,' he said. 'Either it was never there in the first place . . .'

'Or someone's already found it and dug it up,' finished Robert.

Jake felt gloomy as they returned to their cars again.

'This isn't going well,' he whispered to Robert.

'Two down, still two to go,' said Robert confidently.

'Yes, but say we don't find a book?'

'Then we try again another time,' said Robert.

'Maybe the dog's got a cold or a blocked nose?' Jake whispered, shooting a look at Woody; but he knew he was clutching at straws.

He glanced towards Michelle, who was walking ahead of them, chatting to Andy. Jake suspected she was preparing a story for her magazine about sniffer dogs.

'If we don't find one this time, I can't see Michelle spending any more time on this,' he said, worried. 'And we need her to publicise it.'

'You give up too easily, Jake,' said Robert. 'Think positive.'

Jake sighed. It was hard to think positive. He'd been so full of expectations when they'd been planning this. He was sure that Michelle was right, that there would be some of the books buried near to the site of the abbey. And Lauren had been meticulous in her research, locating potential sites for the hidden books.

When they got to the lay-by, Jake looked around at the few cars that were parked there. No blue Renault. And none of the other vehicles looked familiar. Which didn't mean that they weren't being followed, just that someone was being very careful about doing it.

When they arrived at the third site, it looked the same as the first two. Another large field, this one had maize growing in it, and hedgerows left wild all the way around the outside: long grasses, flowers, brambles and nettles.

This is a waste of time, thought Jake gloomily. We've come all this way and we're going to find nothing.

Once again, Andy held the piece of old blackened leather to Woody's nose, and then let the dog amble along the narrow track at the side of the field on the lead, nose to the ground and sniffing, with Jake, Robert and Michelle following. As before, Jake and Robert were carrying spades and a trowel, ready to start digging. They'd gone for only about a hundred metres, when Woody stopped, looked up at Andy and barked excitedly.

'He's found something!' Andy grinned. 'I told you!'

'Is it a book?' asked Michelle eagerly.

'We won't know until we dig it up,' replied Andy.

Woody now ran in small circles excitedly, nose to the ground.

'He's definitely found something!' said Andy proudly. He pulled on the lead, and Woody moved back to sit beside Andy, looking up happily at his master as Andy patted him on the head. Both dog and man almost glowed with pride.

'Right,' said Jake, and he pushed a stout twig into the centre of the spot where Woody had been sniffing so energetically. 'Let's start digging.'

'One at a time,' advised Robert, 'or we could end up getting in each other's way.'

'OK,' said Jake, 'I'll start.'

He pushed the spade's blade into the soft earth with a mounting feeling of excitement. A book! They were going to find a book! Then a niggle of doubt crept in. Maybe Woody had just found a bone. One thing was for sure, they'd soon find out.

Keep your fingers crossed for us, Lauren, he prayed silently, and turned out the first spadeful of soil.

'Stop that!'

It was a man's voice, commanding and angry.

They turned, and saw a tall man approaching, dressed neatly in a tweed jacket and trousers, and carrying a small briefcase.

He reached them, glared at Jake and demanded, 'What do you think you're doing?'

'Digging,' said Jake.

The man shook his head.

'I'm afraid you can't do that.'

'And who are you?' demanded Jake.

'Eric Weems, clerk to the parish council.'

'We've got permission from the landowner,' said Jake. He turned to Robert, who produced the letter of consent he'd got from the farmer and handed it to the man. Weems scanned it, and then handed it back.

'This letter is from the tenant farmer,' he said. 'This land is owned by a corporation.'

'The farmer said he'd contacted them, and they'd said it was all right,' said Robert.

Weems shook his head.

'He may have told you that, but verbal understandings are not lawful,' he told them. 'You need written authorisation from the corporation to dig on their land. And even then, digging is only permitted in the field area where it is already cultivated for agricultural use.' He gestured to the strip of grass and foliage where they were standing. 'The borders around these fields are protected by environmental and ancient monument legislation.'

'Which means . . . what?' asked Michelle.

'You will need permissions from the Heritage Commission, and the Ancient Sites Executive before you can do any digging in this section of ground. As well as from the local councils, parish and district. And to get those permissions, will require a full judicial review.'

So he's a Watcher, thought Jake. And a good one, too. No need for protests or barricades, just bring in the bureaucratic jungle of legislation.

Jake saw that Michelle was about to bluster at the man, and he stepped in swiftly, giving Weems an apologetic smile.

'Our apologies,' he said. 'We weren't aware. We thought the letter we'd been given was authority enough.'

101

Weems shook his head.

'It isn't,' he said firmly.

'No, we see that now,' said Jake, still keeping a genial friendly expression in his face. 'No problem, we'll leave . . .'

Michelle turned to Jake, angry.

'Leave!' she echoed.

'We don't have an alternative.' Jake shrugged apologetically. 'This gentleman has pointed out to us that we can't dig here until we have the necessary authorisations, so that's what we'll do.' He smiled again at Weems. 'We're obviously disappointed, but we do understand. Do you have a card or something, so we can get in touch with you when we're ready to make the applications to dig?'

Weems seemed slightly taken aback at Jake's compliant attitude, but he recovered. He took a small card from his wallet and handed it to Jake. On it were his name and phone numbers.

'There,' he said. Then his manner softened slightly. 'Thank you for being cooperative in this matter,' he said. 'It can be very difficult with so many people searching for things connected with King Arthur. Unfortunately, on previous occasions, I've encountered a more hostile attitude. Sometimes it's even led to my having to call in the police if people have got particularly difficult.'

I bet you have, thought Jake.

'That's no problem, Mr Weems,' he said. 'We understand.' He turned to the others. 'Right, I suggest we head back to the abbey and see what else they might have about Arthur and the Grail.'

With that, Jake set off towards the gate in the fence. The others hesitated, then hurried after him. Michelle caught up with him first.

'You're not just letting him kick us off the site as easily as that!' she demanded, furious.

'Of course not,' Jake whispered back. 'But the last thing we need is a major row. One thing we now know for sure, him turning up like that means we were in the right place. We'll simply come back later, this evening.'

'But we won't find it again in the dark,' insisted Michelle.

'I'm not saying we leave it till dark, just the kind of time that Mr Weems is sitting down to his supper.'

'But say Weems is suspicious and comes back later?'

'We make sure he doesn't,' said Jake. 'Robert, you know all about planning and stuff.'

'Yes,' Robert nodded.

Jake gave Robert Weems's card.

'Could you give him a ring at home this evening and keep him talking about what it entails for us to submit our applications to all these different organisations he mentioned?'

103

Robert grinned.

'And keep him talking for just long enough for you to dig up whatever's at that spot?'

'Exactly,' said Jake.

Chapter 14

Jake felt a mixture of relief and excitement when they got back to the Grail and Thorn. They'd found the hiding place, he felt sure of it, so now he should be able to relax. But the anticipation of uncovering what lay buried at that spot, maybe finding out that it was just another empty cover and not a book, made him feel sick with tension. He felt so edgy that he knew he couldn't just sit in the pub with the others, nor would he be able to relax in the room that he and Robert shared.

'I'm going out to explore Glastonbury,' he told them after they'd parked the cars. 'Anyone fancy coming with me?'

The others declined: Andy wanted to take Woody for a long run; Robert wanted to read a newspaper and do the crossword, and Michelle said she had some work to catch up on.

'OK,' said Jake. 'We'll meet back here at seven, if that's OK with everyone. Hopefully Weems will be off duty by then and settled down in front of the telly.'

'And ready for my very boring call about local planning regulations.' Robert grinned.

Jake headed into the town. As well as needing to be on the move, he reasoned it was a good idea for him to continue to be seen to be checking out all things Arthurian and keep up their cover. It was as he walked along the high street that he became aware of a couple of hippies he was sure he'd seen before.

Not that there should be anything particularly suspicious about that; after all, the place was full of visitors traipsing around, going in and out of shops and exhibits, and the odds were that people would keep bumping into one another. But there was something not quite right about these particular hippies. For one thing, they were young. Most of the hippies walking around Glastonbury seemed to be of an older generation, as though they had got stuck in a time warp in the 1960s, but their bodies had continued to age, and now they were grey-haired and frail-looking echoes of a time long gone by. But these two, although dressed in clothes from a time when tie-dye and sheepskin may have been cool, looked much, much younger. There was also a sharpness, an alertness about them, about their faces and their eyes, that didn't fit with the laid-back look of their clothes. The same alertness was also in the way they moved; they were nimble on their feet. Not that hippies shouldn't be nimble, but these two looked like people disguised as hippies. The man wore a tie-dye waistcoat over flared blue jeans, and the woman wore a long, shaggy sheepskin coat. Both wore coloured beads around their necks, and the man wore beads wrapped around one wrist. It was all too much, thought Jake.

He wondered if they might have been undercover police officers from the drugs squad. That could explain the discrepancy about how they looked, and how they acted. He tried to remember where he'd seen them before. Then it came to him. They'd been sitting at a table in the garden at the Grail and Thorn when he and Robert had arrived. Jake was sure they'd had drinks on the table with them, but they could have been empty glasses, or belonged to someone else. Then he was sure he'd seen them when he'd done his earlier solo walk around Glastonbury.

Had it just been coincidence? Or had Robert been right when he'd said that whoever was watching them would already be at Glastonbury, waiting for them? Had this couple been waiting for them? If so, why hadn't they followed them when they'd gone to dig in the fields?

Jake stopped outside a shop selling crystals and other Arthurian artefacts and examined the display in the window. He stood there for at least three minutes. Then he turned and looked along the street. The couple were still in the same place he'd last seen them, standing outside a café, seemingly reading the menu on display.

Jake headed away from them, along the high street, and as he did he was aware of them moving off after him. Again, it could be coincidence, but there was one way to find out.

Jake did a U-turn and began to head back the way he'd just come, heading straight towards the couple. They stopped and began to look in a shop window as he passed them. Jake headed towards the same café where he'd seen them standing and apparently weighing up the contents of the menu. He went as if he was going to go in, but instead suddenly crossed the road and headed down a narrow cobbled side street, following a side that read 'Public Toilets'.

The public toilets were in a small block in a little garden-like area at the end of the narrow alley. A wooden bench was near them. Jake went to the bench and sat down on it, and as he did so he was sure he saw a flash of light-blue flared jeans appear at the end of the narrow alleyway, but then disappear out of sight. Jake jumped up and headed back towards the alley. The man with the tie-dye waistcoat was standing there. There was no sign of the woman in the sheepskin coat.

The man hesitated. Jake guessed he was upset at being caught out like this. Then the man hurried towards the toilet block and went into the gents.

Again, it could have been coincidence, there weren't that many public toilets in Glastonbury, but Jake was sure the man had been following him and had been forced to go into the toilet to avoid blowing his cover.

So where was the woman? Maybe waiting at the far end of the alley, by the cafeteria, ready to pick Jake up and continue following him if he reappeared. Well, he wasn't going to give her that satisfaction. If she wanted to follow him, she'd have to work a bit harder. Jake crossed the small patch of garden area and headed for another narrow cobbled alley, this one leading towards a Pilgrimage Centre, according to the signpost. Not that it really mattered, Jake reflected. After all, the couple knew Jake and the others were staying at the Grail and Thorn and could pick them up at any time.

Jake wondered who they were, and who they were working for? His instinct was that they were working for Gareth, a pair of MI5 spooks checking that Jake really was in Glastonbury on a quest for King Arthur. Well, they'd be able to report back that Jake had spotted them and given them the slip. Not that he thought they would. After all, they wouldn't want to look bad to their superiors, and — as Jake had said — they knew where everyone was.

But say they *weren't* working for Gareth and MI5? If that was the case, who were they working for?

Chapter 15

When they met up in the pub car park at seven that evening, Jake told the others about the hippie couple, and him giving them the slip. Michelle was dismissive.

'Maybe he really did want to use the toilet in a hurry,' she said. 'Hippies need to pee, too.'

Robert shook his head.

'I think Jake's right,' he said. 'We always guessed we were going to be watched when we got here.' He grinned. 'I just think they got it wrong using that sort of disguise. From Jake's description, I remember seeing the pair of them in the garden when we arrived and thinking they looked like they were going to a fancy dress party. Not the best outfits to wear if you want to keep a low profile and not be spotted.'

'Why all the interest in us?' asked Andy.

'Because of what we're looking for,' said Jake.

Andy shook his head in awe.

'This must be some very special sort of book,' he commented.

Michelle looked at her watch. 'And the sooner we get our hands on it, the better,' she said.

They pulled into the lay-by by the field at half past seven. No one followed them, and there was no further sign of the hippie couple. Jake wondered if the couple had realised they'd been spotted by Jake and had been pulled off the case. In which case, who had taken their place?

As the others got out of the cars, Robert dialled Weems's number.

'Mr Weems,' said Robert cheerfully. 'Robert George calling. We met earlier with my friends in a field.'

Then, while Robert continued the conversation, outlining a hypothetical planning situation and asking complicated questions that would require a whole series of long answers, Jake, Michelle, and Andy with Woody in tow, took spades and a trowel from the boot of the car and headed down the narrow track to the place where Woody had got so excited earlier.

'We'd better be quick,' said Michelle. 'Weems is going to get suspicious if Robert talks for too long, and the next thing we'll have the police on us.'

As before, Jake let the dog sniff at the old oiled book cover, and Woody immediately went straight to the same spot and began barking and turning in a circle.

'Definitely the place.' Andy nodded.

Andy pulled Woody to one side, and the two kept watch for anyone approaching, while Jake set to work, digging, with Michelle filming the whole process.

After a few minutes of digging, with no success, Jake felt his arms tiring and his back aching.

'There's nothing here,' he announced bitterly.

'There is,' said Andy confidently. 'Woody's never wrong. You need to put more welly into it. Dig deeper.'

'And faster,' said Michelle, focusing her camera on the hole that Jake had excavated. 'Robert can't keep Weems talking for ever.'

Jake grimaced, then returned to the task. Despite the urgings to go faster from Michelle and Andy, Jake dug carefully; worried in case the blade of his spade might puncture the leather casing around the book and release whatever might be inside. The image of the man who'd turned into a vegetable at the construction site in Bedfordshire still haunted him.

'There it is!' said Michelle excitedly.

On hearing her exclamation, Andy hurried over, keen to see what was happening. Jake stopped digging and peered into the hole. Yes, there did appear to be something poking out from the earth. He dropped the spade to one side and picked up the trowel, and began to carefully scrape around the dark object he could see. Gradually, a shape was revealed: a small

113

box-like rectangular shape. Jake scraped away more of the earth, and finally exposed a black leather packet embossed with a letter M with a snake writhing through the letter. The symbol of Malichea. He'd found it! He'd found one of the books!

'Stand away and put your hands in the air!'

They all turned, and saw two men standing glaring at them, one old and one young. They looked like father and son. The older of them was holding a shotgun pointed directly at Jake.

Woody may be a great dog for sniffing out things, but he wasn't much of a watchdog, thought Jake bitterly. But even as he thought it, Woody growled and bared his teeth, and Jake was sure that if the dog hadn't been held tightly on a lead, he'd have hurled himself at the man with the gun. Andy made a clicking noise with his tongue, and the dog settled down, but kept his eyes all the time on the man with the gun.

'Hand it over,' snapped the man with the shotgun.

'Hand what over?' asked Jake, looking up at the men from his position inside the hole.

The man with the shotgun scowled.

'That thing you've just dug up,' he said grimly.

As Jake straightened up and turned to face them, stepping out of the hole, he slid the package down inside the back of his jeans.

'We haven't found anything yet,' he insisted.

114

'Don't lie to me,' grunted the older man. 'Just hand it over.'

'Do you have a licence for that shotgun?' asked Andy, speaking with a note of confidence in his voice that surprised Jake.

The older man frowned.

'Yes I do, as a matter of fact,' he said. 'And you're trespassing and illegal treasure hunting. This is my land.'

'We've got permission to dig from the landowner,' put in Michelle.

'That don't matter,' snapped back the older man. 'This was my land before they took it over and there's things here that belong to me and mine.'

He's a Watcher, thought Jake. Weems must have alerted him after he found us.

'That may be,' said Andy, 'but we're not here for treasure.' He reached into his pocket and produced an identification card. 'Search and rescue, working with the police. We're looking for evidence of a crime.'

The older man looked at them, puzzled, and Jake noticed the look of concern that crossed the young man's face.

'What crime?' asked the older man.

'That's official business,' said Andy crisply. 'And at the moment you're committing another one, pointing a loaded gun at plain-clothes police officers.'

'It ain't loaded!' burst out the young man.

'Shut up!' barked the older man at him.

So, thought Jake, definitely Watchers, come to scare us off and stop the book being taken, but not using real violence; just a threat.

Andy pushed his ID card at the young man.

'Take a proper look at that if you don't believe me,' he said.

The young man took Andy's ID card, looked at it, and compared the photograph on the card with Andy, then offered it towards the older man.

'That's what it says, Dad,' he said. 'Search and rescue.'

As I thought, father and son, mused Jake. Handing down the Watcher tradition.

The older man spat on the ground.

'Cards like them don't mean anything,' he said. 'People make 'em up on computers.'

'There's a phone number on it,' said Andy. 'Phone and check. And then put down that gun and let us get on with the job we're here to do.'

The old man looked uncertain, and very unhappy. His son looked even unhappier.

Jake let out a deep sigh which made everyone look at him.

'It's not here,' he said, looking into the hole. 'Looks like our information was wrong. If it was really here, we'd have found it by now.' He shook his head. 'Guess we'd better get back to the station and tell the boss the bad news.'

'What you looking for?' asked the younger man, curious.

'Official business,' said Andy again curtly. 'Need to know.'

'So, we're giving up?' asked Michelle.

Jake nodded.

'Guess so,' he said. 'We'd better go and file our report — "Waste of time".'

With that, he bent down and picked up the spade and trowel.

'Aren't you going to arrest them for threatening us with a shotgun?' asked Andy.

'We weren't threatening!' said the younger man, repeating: 'It's not loaded!'

'It's still threatening,' said Andy coldly.

'We'll let it go this time,' said Jake. He shrugged. 'To be honest, I can't be bothered filling in all the paperwork.'

With that, he set off along the track, carrying the tools, aware of the book pushed down the back of his jeans, and hoping the two men hadn't spotted it. Behind him, he heard Andy tell the two men firmly: 'You've been warned. Do that sort of thing again and you'll be in court.'

Then Andy and Woody followed Jake, with Michelle bringing up the rear. All the time they walked, Jake was aware of the eyes of the two men on them. As they neared the cars, he whispered under his breath to Andy: 'Plain-clothes police?'

Andy chuckled.

'It worked, didn't it?'

Chapter 16

The whole way on the drive back to the Grail and Thorn, Jake sat clutching the black parcel tightly in his hands and staring at it. They'd found one! It was only small, about the size of a thin paperback, but it was real and solid and in his possession!

'What are you going to do with it?' asked Michelle.

'Do what we said, get it tested in a lab, and then you can do a story on it.'

'Yes, but before then. What are you going to do with it *now*?'

'Put it somewhere very safe,' said Jake. This was Lauren's ticket to freedom, and there was no way he was going to let it vanish.

When they got back to the hotel, Jack hurried to the room he shared with Robert, while Robert went off to the bar with Michelle and Andy.

Jake sat on the bed and studied the package. As well

as the letter 'M', the symbol of Malichea, there was a number on it in Roman numerals, but he couldn't quite make them out, and he didn't want to start scraping at it, or do anything that might damage the covering. There was still the problem of potential toxins being inside the book, or even inside the package. He looked at it again. The package was small and closed shut with a knotted leather thong. It looked safe enough, so long as it remained shut.

He looked around the room. Where could he hide it? In his bag? In the bathroom? He dismissed all those options. Those two men, the Watchers, knew they had dug it up. Or, they soon would. Jake was sure they'd come after it. They'd trace them to this hotel. The men were local. They were bound to know someone who worked here. Some money handed over would get them the key to the room. No, Jake couldn't leave it here.

He went to his bag and took out the small first-aid box he always took with him when he went away. He took off his jacket and shirt, slipped the ancient packet inside a small plastic bag, and then taped the bag to his stomach with surgical tape. Luckily, the package was small, and if he wore his shirt hanging loose outside his trousers, hopefully no one would notice. And, if they did, he hoped they'd be polite enough not to tell him he was developing a pot belly.

He stood up and looked at himself in the mirror. The bulge beneath his shirt didn't show.

'Good,' he murmured to himself, satisfied.

He put his jacket on, and went downstairs.

'I can't believe I sat on the phone all that time talking to Weems about planning regulations, and it made no difference!' said Robert.

Jake, Robert and Michelle were sitting at a table in the pub restaurant, relaxing over a beer after their meal. Andy was out, taking Woody for a late-night walk before they all retired to bed. Robert was still brooding on the fact that he'd kept Weems talking at great length, and the Watchers had still turned up to try and disrupt their dig.

'I should have said about how the Watchers work in groups,' admitted Jake. 'Weems couldn't protect that book all on his own. It had to be shared.'

'And all the time he was talking to me about planning requirements, he must have known I was just doing it to keep him talking, and he was quite happy because it was all on my phone bill!' Robert scowled as he took another sip of wine. 'He must have been laughing up his sleeve at me!'

'He won't be laughing when he and his friends realise that we've got the book.' Michelle smiled. She looked at Jake. 'Is it safe?'

'Very safe,' Jake reassured her.

He felt elated. They'd found one of the books! Once they got back to London, Michelle would talk to her editor and show him the film she'd taken on her camera, and then the process could start rolling about putting the hidden library of Malichea right into the eye of the public. No more secrets, no more mysteries kept hidden, just open transparency. The truth would be out there, and Lauren could come home. Maybe not immediately, but soon.

'My room's been turned over!'

The three turned to see Andy, standing with Woody beside him on his lead. Andy looked furious.

'What?' asked Michelle.

'I've just been up to my room to put Woody in after our walk, and my room's been ransacked,' said Andy. 'Someone's gone through everything. My stuff's all over the floor.'

Robert and Michelle turned to look at Jake, shocked, and then they all headed upstairs to their rooms.

They found them in the same state as Andy's: in the room that Jake and Robert shared, their suitcases had been opened and then left lying upside down on the floor, with their clothes strewn around. It was the same in Michelle's room: her overnight bag open and dumped, and her clothes thrown on to the floor.

And none of the locks of the doors have been damaged, noticed Jake. So either someone had picked the locks, or it had been done by someone using a pass-key. If it was a pass-key, then Jake guessed it could have been the two men they'd encountered with the shotgun, the Watchers. If the locks had been picked, then they were up against someone much more dangerous.

'They were looking for the book,' said Michelle. 'Those two must have dug into the hole after we'd gone and discovered it wasn't there, and they came looking for it.'

'Or it was someone else,' muttered Jake.

'What?' asked Michelle.

'Who?' demanded Andy.

'There have been other people trying to find it,' said Jake. 'Before we came down here. They tried to stop us.'

'They slashed Lizzie's tyres!' growled Robert, still angry at the memory.

Andy looked puzzled.

'You mean that those two blokes were in London?' he said, baffled.

'No,' said Jake. 'These were other people.'

Andy let out a low whistle.

'Like I said, this must really be some special book!' he said.

'I'm not happy about staying here tonight,' announced Jake.

'Why?' asked Michelle. 'If it was those two gaffers we met who did this, they didn't seem particularly harmful. OK, they tried to threaten us with a gun, but it wasn't loaded, and when Andy did that thing with his ID card, they backed down.'

'But say it wasn't them?' said Jake. 'Say someone followed us down from London. The people who slashed Robert's tyres.' And who stuck that picture of Lauren on my wall with a knife, thought Jake miserably. 'Trust me, not everyone who's after the books is harmless. And if we stay here, who knows what they might do tonight to get hold of the book.' He gestured at the mess in the rooms. 'This is nothing. I've seen what these people can do.' And, with a shudder, he remembered finding the body of the ex-SAS soldier in his flat, stabbed to death.

'Well, I can't leave,' said Robert. 'I've had enough wine to stop me driving tonight.'

'And there's no way I'm taking a chance of driving anywhere and losing my licence,' put in Michelle.

Jake sighed. If he stayed here tonight he was in danger, and he knew it.

'Maybe there's a train back to London?' suggested Robert.

Michelle shook her head.

'No,' she said. 'I checked it out before I came down here, just in case I could do it by train. There's no station at Glastonbury, and I think you'll have missed the last train from the nearest place.' She checked her watch, and nodded. 'Yes. No last train for you.' She shrugged. 'Looks like you're here till the morning.'

'Oh dear,' said Andy. They looked at him, and he gave them all a rueful grin. 'This is where the non-drinker always suffers. A weekend party, a match, an outing, guess who gets to be the designated driver.' He looked at Jake and asked: 'How serious is it? This threat you're talking about?'

'Very serious,' said Jake. 'I'm not joking.'

Andy hesitated, then said, 'You sure you can't wait till the morning?'

Robert looked at Andy, shocked.

'You're not seriously thinking of driving back to London with Jake tonight?' he asked, incredulous.

Andy shrugged.

'Well, you and Michelle can't do it. And if Jake thinks there's a real threat . . .'

'I do,' said Jake firmly. Then he softened. 'No, Andy, it's not fair. After all, you don't know me, except through Robert . . . and I know it's asking a bit much for you to drive me all the way back in the middle of the night.'

'But this book is important, right?' asked Andy. 'Getting it safe?'

'Yes.' Jake nodded.

'OK,' said Andy. 'Give me time to stuff my things back in my bag and get Woody sorted out, and we'll go.'

Jake felt a wave of relief wash over him. What a great bloke! But then, he supposed that was the kind of unselfish person you found in search and rescue, someone who thought nothing of putting themselves at risk for others. A pity there aren't more Andys in this world, thought Jake.

'Thanks, Andy,' he said. 'I promise, some day, I'll pay you back for doing this. I don't know how, but I will.'

Chapter 17

Late at night, there was hardly any traffic on the road as they headed east, so they made good time. Jake sat in the passenger seat, feeling the book still taped to his stomach, and relieved to be away from Glastonbury. He had no doubt that whoever was after the book would have struck again that night, and not just ransacking a room.

Behind Jake, Woody lay in the footwell of the back seat. It also gave Jake comfort, that, if they were suddenly overtaken and their car stopped, they had the dog with them to defend them. Jake had already seen the dog prepared to launch an attack when that shotgun had been pointed at them.

As they drove, Andy talked about his search and rescue work, and then he asked about the book they'd found, and what it was all about.

'Robert didn't tell me a lot about it,' he said.

So Jake told him about the Order of Malichea, and monks hiding the library, and all the different people who were trying to get their hands on the books. It helped pass the time on the long drive, and Jake felt he owed it to Andy, especially as he was putting himself out this way.

'So that's why you wanted to head back to London,' said Andy. 'To get the book back there to safety.'

'Right,' agreed Jake. 'The way they'd searched our rooms for it meant to me they'd try again.'

'Makes sense,' said Andy.

Ahead of them, they saw the sign for a twenty-four-hour service station.

'Excellent,' said Andy. 'We could do with some petrol. And I don't know about you, but a coffee would help keep me awake on the rest of the journey.'

'Sounds a great idea,' said Jake.

Andy signalled, and pulled into the service station. Ahead of them, the cafeteria was lit up, but there were few cars parked. Jake wasn't surprised; at this time of night he didn't expect there to be much traffic. Andy ignored the service station and turned into the lorry park, where rows and rows of lorries were parked up for the night.

'You missed it,' said Jake.

'Missed what?' asked Andy.

'The car park. This is the lorry park.'

'I know,' said Andy. 'But this is quieter. Fewer people around.'

Jake frowned.

'You think someone might steal your car?' he asked.

'No,' said Andy. 'But I need you to hand the book over, and if you resist, it might get noisy.'

Jake stared at Andy, bewildered. Andy still seemed the same easy-going guy he'd been all weekend, but there was a harder look to his expression that hadn't been there before. Cold.

'What do you mean? I don't understand,' said Jake, still trying to come to terms with what Andy was saying.

'I mean you're going to hand the book over to me.'

'Why?'

'Because someone is paying me thirty thousand pounds to get hold of it.'

'Thirty thousand?'

Andy nodded.

'Someone has obviously been listening in to yours and Robert's conversations, because I got this phone call from someone who knew that Robert had asked me to go to Glastonbury with you. They told me you were looking for some sort of book. Well, I knew that, because Robert had already told me. Then they told me they'd pay me thirty thousand if I could get hold of it.

'They paid me ten thousand in cash up front as a sign of good faith, and told me I could keep it, whatever happened. But, if I could get hold of the book, there was another twenty thousand in it for me.'

'But you're Robert's friend!' exploded Jake.

'I play rugby in the same team as him,' corrected Andy. 'It's not the same thing.'

'So . . . was it you who searched our rooms?'

Andy nodded.

'But your own room was searched as well,' said Jake, bewildered.

'Of course,' said Andy. 'I had to make it look good.' He grinned. 'When you got all jumpy and said you had to get back to London tonight . . . well . . . That was better than I imagined.'

Jake stared at Andy, his mind still in shock. He'd been so friendly, so helpful. And now . . .

'I can't let you have it,' he said.

'It's not a question of *can't*,' said Andy. 'It's a question of what will happen to you if you don't.' He gave a low whistle, and suddenly Jake heard the dog growl. 'Good old Woody,' said Andy. 'Like I say, a nice friendly dog. Except when he thinks his master's in danger, or being attacked. Then, he's a different animal. He'd tear your throat out if he thought you were threatening me.'

'But I'm not!' said Jake desperately.

'If I give that whistle, he'll think you are,' said Andy. 'It's a sort of code between us, something we've developed.' He smiled. 'Working dogs are very close to their masters, and vice versa. They'll kill for them. Now . . . do you hand over the book, or do I get Woody to tear you apart and I'll search through the pieces?' He shrugged. 'I don't think the people who are paying me mind if there's blood on it when I hand it over.'

'I haven't got it,' said Jake desperately.

Andy shook his head.

'Don't try that with me, Jake,' he said. 'You've just told me you have. So why mess about and get hurt? Just hand it over, and that's it. We'll call it a day. After all, you can always find another one.'

'I can't,' said Jake. 'I need it. This book is the only way to get someone's who's very important to me back here. Without it, we're sunk.'

Andy sighed.

'If that's the way you want to play it,' he said. And he gave the same low whistle again, longer this time, and this time the dog growled deep in its throat, and then suddenly leapt up at Jake, snapping at the back of his head. Jake threw himself forward, but he felt the dog's hot breath and the saliva on his hair.

Andy made a clicking sound with his tongue and Woody settled back down.

'He'll tear your scalp off and then your face,' said Andy. 'Save yourself the pain, I would. Give it up. And don't think about running. Woody will catch you, he's fast.'

He saw Jake shoot a glance out at the rows of lorries parked up.

'And don't think you can hide in that lot. You saw yourself how good Woody's sense of smell is. He'll find you. Now . . . hand it over.'

Jake hesitated, then asked, 'How do I know you won't set the dog on me after I've given it to you?'

'Because it won't be necessary,' said Andy. 'I'm not interested in hurting you for the sake of it, I'm only interested in getting my hands on the rest of the money. You give me the book. I leave you here and drive off. You can get a lift from someone, or phone a taxi, or whatever. I don't care. All I want is the book.'

Jake sagged in the passenger seat, a defeated look on his face.

'OK,' he said. He tapped the front of his jacket. 'It's strapped to my chest.'

'A good hiding place,' said Andy. 'Now, take it out and hand it over. And remember, no tricks. Woody's just behind you, and he's very fast.'

Jake nodded. He unzipped his jacket, and then started to unbutton his shirt, fumbling as he did.

'Faster,' said Andy.

'The dog makes me nervous,' complained Jake.

'That's why he's here,' said Andy. 'Come on, hurry up.'

Chapter 18

Jake undid another button, and suddenly he swung to his left and pressed down on the door handle and threw himself out of the car. Immediately, he heard Andy whistle, and the dog growl fiercely. He saw a blur of fur hurtling towards him from the back of the car, saw the dog's open mouth, his fangs threatening in the ambient light, the dog's front paws hitting the ground. Then Jake slammed the door hard.

There was a sickening crunch of metal on bone, and a howl of pain from the dog. Then Jake was running, heading for the rows of trucks. Behind him he heard a car door open, but there was no sound of the dog coming after him, just a continuous howl of pain.

'I'll get you!' came the enraged shout from Andy.

By then, Jake had reached the first of the rows of lorries, and he dodged in between two of them.

He made his way between the massive trucks, searching desperately for a loose tarpaulin that meant he could climb up and hide, but most were fastened securely. Others were tankers, with no place to conceal himself. Then he saw one open flatbed truck piled with palettes. Quickly, he hauled himself up, and crawled in between the stacks of palettes.

He heard the sound of a car boot slamming shut, and then Andy calling out angrily: 'I'm going to kill you for what you did to Woody!'

Jake peered out and saw Andy heading for the lorries. Something metallic glinted in his hand. A tyre lever, Jake guessed.

'I'm going to find you and beat you to a pulp!' roared Andy, and there was no mistaking the fury in his voice. Easy-going Andy was gone completely, in his place was an enraged and armed vengeful man with one thought in his mind: to get Jake.

Jake held his breath, terrified in case Andy might hear the rasp of fear in his throat. As he watched, Andy stood stock still, his head swivelling left and right as he scanned the lorries. He was obviously working out which ones Jake couldn't be hiding in, and which were possibles.

Andy turned away from the tankers, and the closed container lorries, and then his eyes lit on the open flat-bed piled high with palettes, and he headed straight for it, the weapon swinging in his hand.

Jake ducked down, frantically wondering what to do. He could jump down and make a run for it, but he was fairly sure that Andy was fitter and faster than he was. Andy was also driven by wanting revenge for Jake injuring his dog, but most of all, by the further twenty thousand pounds the book offered.

Jake pushed himself down as low as he could, his face pressed into the wooden boards of the flatbed. He heard Andy's boots getting nearer and nearer. He's here! thought Jake in alarm. He's going to climb up and find me!

But suddenly the truck's engine started up. The flatbed throbbed with the engine's vibrations. The driver must have decided to get going.

The truck pulled away. *Please don't let him stop for fuel*, prayed Jake silently. But the truck didn't, it headed towards the exit, and the slip road on to the main route east. Jake took a quick glance back at the lorry park, and saw Andy was still searching among the lorries, bending down and looking beneath them. Which meant he wouldn't be chasing after them.

Jake let himself relax briefly, but then tensed up again as the truck began to shake from side to side. He fixed himself firmly between two stacks of palettes, wedging himself in with the soles of his feet, to make sure he didn't slide to the edge of the truck. Then he pulled out his mobile phone and dialled Robert. It took a while before Robert answered, and when he did, he didn't sound happy.

'Do you know what time it is?' Robert demanded. It was obvious that Jake's call had woken him up.

'Yes,' said Jake. 'Robert, I'm in trouble.'

Quickly, he told him what had happened between him and Andy.

'Where are you now?' said Robert, shocked. 'What's all that noise in the background?'

'I'm on the back of a lorry,' said Jake. 'I think it's heading towards London, but I don't know. I just hope it isn't going too far away.'

'You could end up on the Continent,' said Robert.

'In that case it'd have to stop at a port,' pointed out Jake. 'I could end up in Scotland. The point is, Robert, we can't trust Andy. He tried it on me. He might try it on you.'

'Oh no he won't!' said Robert determinedly. 'Anyway, why should he? He knows you've got the book.'

'Yes, but he might use you to get to me,' said Jake.

'OK,' said Robert. 'Thanks for the warning.' And he added vengefully: 'I have a score to settle with Andy.'

'I'll phone you tomorrow, after it's daylight and once I know what's happening,' said Jake. 'Don't phone me. The driver might hear the ring tone coming from the back of his truck. In the meantime, tell Michelle what's happened, and tell her I'll be in contact.'

'Will do,' said Robert. 'And phone me if you need help, or you want me to come and pick you up anywhere.'

'Thanks, Robert. I'm going to keep my fingers crossed I get somewhere safely. I'll talk to you later.'

Chapter 19

The journey seemed to take for ever. Jake felt exhausted but he was too scared to fall asleep in case he slid off the edge of the flatbed as he rattled along through the night. Dawn came, and Jake watched the sun rise. He wondered where the truck was heading. He was sure it had taken a turn northwards, but he couldn't be sure. And, hidden as he was, he couldn't see the road signs. Finally, the truck pulled into another truck stop. Jake waited until he'd heard the sound of the cab door opening and closing, and the driver's footsteps leaving, before he clambered down from the back of the truck. Jake headed towards the cafeteria, where his first call was the toilet, and then a cup of much-needed coffee.

From the sign in the entrance, he discovered that this particular truck stop was just outside Watford. That meant he was a short train ride from Euston, and central London.

He phoned Robert's number, but got voicemail. Next, he tried Michelle's, but that also went straight to her answering service.

From the information board he learnt that there was a bus stop just outside the truck stop which would take him to Watford station, and fifteen minutes later he was on the bus. He'd already decided that keeping the book on him was too dangerous. He'd nearly lost it to Andy. If he was grabbed by anyone, they'd simply take it off him, just as Andy had been going to do. He'd have to hide it somewhere, but where? Not at his flat, that would be too obvious. Not at Robert's, for the same reason. It had to be somewhere anonymous. He decided he'd leave it at the Left Luggage office at Euston.

When he got to Watford station, he went into a shop and bought a small rucksack and a cheap casual jacket. He went to the station toilets, unstrapped the plastic bag containing the book from his stomach, wrapped it inside the casual jacket, then put them both in the rucksack.

He caught the train to Euston, and once there went straight to the Left Luggage office on the concourse and handed in the rucksack. He felt a mixture of relief and trepidation as he walked away; relief that the book was no longer on him and liable to be snatched, but fearful because the book was now semi-exposed.

But then, he reflected, he'd been very careful to make sure he hadn't been followed from Watford. And, even after he put the rucksack into the Left Luggage office, he'd hung around for ten minutes, watching the office in case anyone tried to claim the rucksack. No one did.

Jake went out of the station and tried Robert again. This time, he answered.

'Jake! Where are you?'

'Back in London. Where are you?'

'I'm at the car hire company, returning the car. Then I'm going home to sort Lizzie out.'

'OK. I'll go home first to get freshened up, then I'll see you at your place,' said Jake.

'What about the *thing*?' asked Robert.

'It's safe,' said Jake. 'I'll tell you when I see you.'

Jake felt uneasy as he left Finsbury Park station and headed towards his block of flats. For once he'd taken the tube rather than the bus. The whole time he had a sense of being watched. Don't be ridiculous, he told himself. If anyone had been following you, you'd have noticed them on the tube train. But would he have? He'd read somewhere that spies worked in teams when following someone to avoid being spotted. So, just in case he was being tracked, he made sure to stop every

141

now and then and looked around, seeing if any of the people behind him, or on the other side of the road, looked familiar.

He made it back to his small block of flats without trouble, but as he turned the corner of his street he saw something that sent a jolt of fear through him, and made him duck back immediately. Andy's car was there, parked in the street near his flats.

He's going to kill me, thought Jake. He's going to kill me because of what I did to his dog. And, before he does, who knows what he's going to do to me to find out where the book is.

Carefully, Jake peered out from behind the corner building towards Andy's car. Was Andy inside it? Or was he lurking, hiding in a doorway somewhere, ready to pounce as soon as Jake appeared? He strained his eyes. The car seemed to be empty, but as he looked he saw a movement inside by the driver's headrest. Yes, Andy was inside the car. He guessed Andy's attention was fully focused on the entrance to his block of flats.

Jake turned and headed back the way he'd come, towards Finsbury Park station. He could phone Robert and get him to come over and deal with Andy, but Jake didn't want to hang around any longer than was necessary. As Jake walked, he dialled Robert's number on his phone. There was no answer, just voicemail. Jake assumed Robert was still sorting out the damage to his van, Lizzie.

It was a long way to go, all the way from Finsbury Park to Robert's house at Baron's Court, and Jake considered other options: contacting Michelle and seeking help from her; or maybe even phoning the police and accusing Andy of stalking him. But Michelle only wanted the book to publicise it; and Andy would just claim he was waiting for a friend. No, the only safe place Jake could think of right at this moment was Robert's house.

When Jake arrived at Robert's neat terraced house, the old van was still parked on the tiny forecourt, its four tyres still flat. So Robert hadn't managed to get the damage repaired yet. Jake went to the door and rang the bell.

Usually, Robert opened the door almost as soon as the bell had sounded, but today there was no response. Maybe Robert was out, talking to a tyre company, negotiating a deal to get Lizzie back on the street.

Jake rang the bell again.

'Come on, Robert,' he muttered impatiently to himself. He didn't fancy exposing himself on this doorstep for any longer than was necessary. With so many people after him, who knew who might be watching.

He gave a bang on the door with his knuckles. As he did, the door swung inwards. Immediately, Jake felt alarm bells ringing in his head. Why was the door unlocked? Jake stayed outside and peered into the house, into the long hallway, his ears straining for any sound.

'Robert!' he called.

There was no answer.

Something was wrong. Robert wouldn't go out and leave his front door open and unlocked, he was far too careful for that.

'Robert!' Jake called again, louder this time.

There was still no answer.

Warily, Jake entered the house, all his senses alert for any sound or movement. His heart thumped loudly in his chest, adding to his feeling of controlled panic. Was there someone waiting for him, waiting to pounce? But if so, why wait? Surely they'd have come out at him already, as soon as he walked in.

The first door on his left was the small living room. Carefully, slowly, Jake put his fingertips against the door and pushed it open. Nothing happened. No one rushed out at him. He looked into the room. It was empty, everything was in its proper place, everything neat and tidy. No sign of any disturbance.

Jake moved back into the hallway and moved on, still quietly, still listening intently. Next was the kitchen. The door was already half open. Jake entered, and stopped dead, in shock. Robert was tied to a wooden chair, his clothes torn and stained with blood. Blood had run down from a gash on his scalp and was starting to congeal on Robert's face. He was deathly still, only held upright by the ropes that tied him to the back of the chair.

Jake hurried over and put his fingers to Robert's neck, and felt a faint pulse.

'Robert!' said Jake.

There was no response.

Jake looked at Robert's bruised and battered face and felt a mixture of fury and nausea rise up in him. He pulled out his mobile and tapped out 999. Urgently, he gave Robert's address to the operator.

'He's been attacked,' he told her. 'He needs an ambulance and paramedics urgently.'

'Your name, please?' asked the operator.

'John Smith,' replied Jake. 'Please, hurry. He may be dying.'

Then he clicked off the phone and headed back out through the hallway and out to the street. There was nothing he could do for Robert right now. He didn't know how badly he was damaged, what sort of internal injuries he might have. If Jake tried to take him out of the chair it might make them worse.

Jake crossed the road, walked along to a nearby bus stop and joined the short queue, his eyes on Robert's house. All he could do for Robert was wait to make sure the paramedics turned up, and if they didn't, phone again.

He stood at the bus stop for five minutes, checking his watch and getting more and more agitated as he waited for the emergency services to arrive, aware that every second that passed meant Robert could be slipping further into danger. Finally, he heard the sound of the sirens approaching, then an ambulance appeared at the far end of the street and screeched to a halt outside Robert's house. A police car was close behind it.

Relieved, Jake waited until he saw the medics and police hurry into the house, then he slipped away from the crowd waiting for the bus and headed towards the tube station. *Please let Robert be all right*, he prayed silently. *Let him live. Let him recover. Let him return to full health.*

Whoever had done that to Robert had thought he had the book, or that he knew where it was. Who? Not the people that Andy had been hired by, surely. Andy had known that Jake had the book on him. Unless the people who had beaten up Robert had been looking for Jake and were trying to force Robert to tell them where Jake was.

At the thought of Robert, tied to the chair, bloody and unconscious, Jake shuddered. These people would stop at nothing. They wanted the book. If they caught him, they'd do the same to him as they'd done to Robert. He had to get the book to Michelle. There was no time to wait. He had to make sure she went public with it *now*.

He dialled Michelle's number, but just got voice-mail. Where was she? Why wasn't she answering? The awful thought struck him that the people who'd beaten Robert up so badly had got to her. In which case, they could well be watching the offices of the magazine where she worked, waiting for him to show up.

I'm caught, he realised. I can't go home. I can't go to Michelle's office. I can't stay around Robert's house.

He headed into the tube station and got on an east-bound train back towards the city centre. He had to hide; and the best place to hide was in a place filled with people. Safety in numbers, while he worked out what he was going to do next.

Chapter 20

As Jake came out of the entrance of Tottenham Court Road station into Oxford Street, his mobile rang. Michelle calling him back? He looked at the screen: number withheld, but it could still be Michelle.

'Hello?' he said.

It was Gareth.

'All right, Jake. Bring it to me.'

'Bring what?'

'The book you found at Glastonbury, of course.'

'Book?' queried Jake.

Gareth exploded in anger.

'For heaven's sake, you didn't think I was that gullible to believe you'd suddenly developed a major interest in all things King Arthur, did you? We knew what you were up to, but we decided to let you go ahead and keep an eye on you and see if you turned up anything. And look what happens! Your friend,

Robert, for example. In a coma with a fractured skull.'

As he heard these words, Jake felt sick.

'Is he going to be all right?' he asked.

Even as he said it, the words felt lame and foolish. Inadequate. Robert had been beaten almost to death, and it was his fault. He had got Robert involved.

'Is he going to die, you mean?' snapped Gareth. 'Frankly, we don't know. The doctors say he's only got a forty per cent chance of surviving. The point is, Jake, the people who did it are still out there, and looking for *you*. You're next. So bring the book to me and stop this now.'

'I haven't got it,' Jake mumbled.

There was a brief pause, then Gareth said, 'Jake, I don't think you understand your position and how much danger you're in, so I'll spell it out for you. Your friend has had his skull crushed. He may well die. They thought he had the book. He didn't. They are now coming after you, and they will kill you unless you give them the book, or tell them where it is. I can protect you. Bring the book to me *now*.'

'All right,' said Jake. He had to play for time. 'I'll bring it to your office.'

Before Gareth could respond, Jake ended the call. Almost immediately, his phone rang.

Michelle, or Gareth calling back, angry at having been cut off?

'Jake Wells,' he said.

'Alex Munro,' said Alex Munro's familiar self-assured voice. 'Your friendly taxi service.'

Jake tensed.

'I'm a bit busy at the moment,' he said. And that's an understatement, he thought.

'Yes, the book you've got,' said Munro in an almost casual way. 'The one you found at Glastonbury.' There was a brief pause, then he added: 'A pity about your friend. I understand he's in a bad way.'

How did Munro know all this so soon? thought Jake. But then he reflected that Pierce Randall had contacts everywhere: in the police, inside the Department of Science, possibly in Gareth's own office.

'Yes he is,' he said grimly, adding angrily: 'and if I find you were behind it . . .'

'No no, Jake, I assure you,' said Munro quickly and smoothly. 'You should know by now that violence is not our style.'

No, but it's the style of some of the people you use, and who you represent, thought Jake. The Mafia and a whole load of other organised criminal gangs, for example.

'You're at serious risk, Jake,' continued Munro. 'I can save you, and give you what you want. Just bring me the book.'

'No,' said Jake. 'This one's going out into the public

150

domain. This one is going to prove to the world that the secret library of Malichea exists.'

'Which is our aim, too, Jake,' said Munro smoothly.

'No it isn't,' snapped back Jake. 'You want to sell this to the highest bidder and keep it secret, just like everyone else. The difference is that you'll patent what's in it and make a fortune from it.'

'You mean you've looked inside it?' said Munro, and now Jake heard a new eagerness in his voice. 'What's the subject matter, Jake? Who's it by?'

Jake hesitated. He was on the point of admitting he didn't know, he hadn't even opened the book, then he stopped himself. Don't give anything away, he told himself. Let Munro think that Jake knew what the contents were. He might need a bargaining chip of some sort in the future.

'Jake, we can help you,' said Munro. 'You want Ms Graham back, we can arrange that. As I told you earlier, dealing with governments is one of our main areas of expertise. Just bring me the book . . .'

'No,' said Jake.

'I understand,' said Munro. 'You're worried about your own safety. So we'll come to you. Just tell me where you are and we'll collect you. We'll send our best people. They'll make sure you're safe . . .'

Suddenly, it hit Jake that Munro knew where he was. He remembered what he'd been told, that people could be tracked by the signal from their mobile phone. Munro was using this call to pinpoint Jake's position. Quite likely, even now, Munro's people were on their way to him. And maybe Gareth's people as well. Gareth's secret services certainly had that same technology.

Fumbling with nervous fingers, Jake opened his mobile phone, took out the battery and SIM card, and slipped them into one pocket, with the dismantled remains of his phone into another. He looked up, and saw a black car pull up about a hundred metres away from him. Two men got out of the back, both dressed in dark suits. Their heads turned swiftly from side to side, scanning the crowds in the street, searching. Plain-clothes police, or secret agents, or Munro's men? It didn't matter, Jake just knew that he had to get away.

He ducked down a side street and found himself heading down one of the short streets that linked Oxford Street with Soho Square. Out of the corner of his eye he was aware of the two men turning towards his direction, just before he nipped into the street. He ran, and as he did he heard shouts of complaints from behind him. The two men were obviously pushing people aside as they gave chase.

Jake ducked down as he ran, hoping to keep out of sight. Were the men armed? Were they the people who'd beaten Robert almost to death?

He ran, pushing people aside himself, desperate to

get away from his pursuers, but the crowd on the street were too busy. His only chance was to run out into the road, but if he did that he risked them getting a clear look at him, and possibly a clear shot.

Suddenly he saw an alley through an archway, just to his right. He ran towards it, and immediately turned right into yet another narrow alleyway, and as he did so he felt a hand grab him.

Fear surged through him and he turned, and came face to face with a short black teenage girl.

'In the dumpster!' she hissed at him.

'What?' said Jake, bewildered.

She punched him so that he turned round, and he saw a teenage boy standing by a tall dumpster, holding a hand ready for him to use as a step.

'Come on, man!' the boy said urgently, in a whisper.

Jake ran to him, put his foot in the boy's open palm, and found himself lifted up, and then falling into the large metal box, landing on a foul-smelling mix of paper, cardboard and rotting vegetables.

Immediately, he heard raised voices from just outside the dumpster, the boy's voice, angry, challenging: 'What you doin' smackin' me like that?'

'I didn't,' came the curt reply.

'Yes you did,' said the boy. 'That's assault, that is. I could bring the law in and have you arrested. Get compensation.'

153

'Shut up,' snapped the man. 'Where did he go?'

'Who?' came the girl's voice.

'The man who ran through that arch,' said another voice, the second man.

'Why you wanna know?' asked the girl.

'That's our business,' said the first man sharply.

'Yeah? Well, that's what this is, *business*!' said the girl firmly. 'How much?'

Oh God, thought Jake, they're going to sell me out! That's what this is about, street kids making money!

There was a pause, then the first man said: 'Here.'

The girl responded with a derisory laugh.

'A fiver!' she said. 'You jokin' me? A *fiver*!'

'We're losing time,' said the second man urgently.

Immediately, the first man said: 'Here.'

The girl said, 'A twenty. That's more like it.' Then, with a smile that Jake heard in her voice, she said: 'You must want him bad. What's he done?'

'Just tell us where he went or I'll have that back!' grated the first man.

'Whoa!' said the girl. 'No need to get crazy.'

No, begged Jake silently. Don't tell them. If I'd known this was about money, I'd have given you every penny.

'He went that way,' said the boy, 'down Dean Street.'

Jake heard a grunt, then the clatter of shoes running off. There was a pause, then a bang on the side of the dumpster. He raised his head and looked down at the boy and girl.

'They gone,' said the boy.

'Thanks,' said Jake.

He struggled to get a grip on the top of the dumpster, and then climbed out and dropped down to the pavement.

'You was lucky we was here,' said the girl.

'I know,' agreed Jake.

'They're cops, right?' said the boy.

'Sort of,' said Jake.

'So what you do?' asked the girl.

'Nothing!' protested Jake.

'Yeah, like the cops is gonna chase you for nothing!' sneered the boy. 'And you wearin' proper good clothes 'an all, not a hoodie or nuthin.'

'Yeah, you ain't street, and they plain clothes, so it's gotta be somethin' heavy.' The girl nodded in agreement. She frowned at Jake suspiciously. 'You a murderer?'

'No I am not!' said Jake vehemently.

'So who are they?' asked the boy. 'Them people chasin' you?'

Jake hesitated. He was about to brush the kids off by saying he didn't know, or it was mistaken identity, but one look at them told him they were too smart for that. And they had saved him, so he owed them.

'They're government agents,' he said.

The kids looked at him, momentarily awed, then the impressed expressions on their faces were replaced with sneering disbelief.

'Yeah!' said the boy, his lip curling, and he spat on the ground. 'Expect me to believe that!'

'It's true!' insisted Jake. 'They tracked me through my mobile phone. I had to take it apart.'

And he reached into his pocket and pulled out the remains of his mobile phone, the battery and SIM card.

The boy and girl exchanged questioning looks. Then they turned back to Jake and the girl demanded: 'So why they chasing you?'

'They think I've got something they want,' said Jake.

'And have you?' asked the girl.

Jake hesitated, then he shook his head.

'No,' he told them, and reflected that it wasn't a lie, the book was still at Euston Left Luggage office. At least, he hoped it was.

'So why you run?' asked the boy. 'Why don't you stop and tell them you ain't got this thing, whatever it is?'

'Because they won't believe me,' said Jake.

The two kids looked at him quizzically. Finally, the girl asked: 'You a spy?'

'Yeah,' the boy nodded, 'that's who he is. He's James Bond.' He grinned. 'Even if he look a wimp.'

'I'm not a wimp!' responded Jake, put out.

'Well, you sure look one,' said the boy.

The girl nodded in agreement.

'Anyway, you owe us,' she said.

'I do,' said Jake humbly. 'And I thank you.'

The girl looked at Jake challengingly.

'You *thank* us?' she echoed. 'You think your thanks is gonna get us a bed for the night, or put food in our bellies?'

Of course, they wanted paying, Jake realised.

'Look, I haven't got much cash on me,' began Jake.

'That's OK, we don't want your money,' cut in the boy.

The girl glared at the boy.

'What you tellin' him that for, fool!' she said angrily. 'Of course we do! You got any money?'

The boy looked uncomfortable.

'That ain't the point,' he said. 'He was on the run from the man. We've all been on the run like that, and we got help when we needed it. People was there for us. That's what this is about. What goes around comes around. You gotta pass it on.'

The girl shook her head and looked at the boy disdainfully.

'You're full of bullshit,' she snapped. 'You bin hanging around them Hare Krishna people too much!'

'I'm just sayin' . . . !' the boy snapped back at her defensively.

'Look, please . . . !' cut in Jake, eager to stop an argument developing between the two.

'You're right, I do owe you. And I want to give you money for helping me.' He took out his wallet and looked inside. He had thirty pounds in ten-pound notes. He took two of them and held them out. 'This is all I've got, except for ten pounds left for me,' he said, and he showed them the inside of his wallet to prove he wasn't lying.

'I don't know . . .' began the boy thoughtfully, but the girl snatched the two ten-pound notes from Jake's fingers.

'I do,' she said firmly.

The boy looked Jake up and down, curious.

'So, what you gonna do now?' he asked.

'Do?' repeated Jake.

'Yeah. Those agent dudes still after you.'

'Easy.' The girl shrugged. 'He's gonna go home and come up with some other story to explain why he's all smelly from being in that dumpster.'

'I can't go home,' said Jake. The girl and the boy looked at him, the boy puzzled, the girl suspicious.

'Why?' asked the boy.

'Because they'll be watching my flat, waiting for me.'

The boy's expression hardened, then he turned to the girl and said, 'We gotta take care of him.'

158

'Oh no!' said the girl quickly. 'Not another of your lame pigeons!'

'Duck,' Jake corrected her automatically.

'What?' she demanded.

'The saying is lame duck,' said Jake. 'Not lame pigeon.'

The girl glared at him, then she said defiantly, 'Well, I ain't never seen no lame duck, but I seen plenty of lame pigeons. So, it's a lame pigeon, right.' And she turned to the boy and said, 'And he's on his own. We ain't takin' care of him.'

'Why?' appealed the boy. He gestured towards Jake. 'Look at him. He's scared. He's messy. He ain't got nowhere to go. He's on the run. This is a man looking for help. It's up to us to help him.'

Jake stared at the boy, and a feeling of amazement came over him. Here were two kids, street kids, he guessed, much younger than him, and they were talking about protecting him, an adult — well, more of an adult than either of these two. He wanted to run away from them and hide, but where? He was adrift and alone on the streets, and until he could get hold of Michelle and get the book to her, he needed help. And here were these two kids, offering that help.

'I'm Jez,' said the boy, 'and this here's Ronnie.'

'I'm Jake,' said Jake, and he held out his hand. The boy, surprised, took it and shook it, then released it.

Ronnie just looked at Jake's proffered hand with a cold eye, as if it was some suspicious thing that was about to bring them bad luck, and sniffed disdainfully again.

She turned to Jez, her expression one of disapproval. 'Guess we got us a lame pigeon,' she said.

Chapter 21

'First thing we gotta do is get you off the street,' said Jez.

'And cleaned up,' added Ronnie. Her nose wrinkled in distaste. 'There was some real stinky stuff in that dumpster.'

'Benjy's,' suggested Jez. He looked at his watch. 'He'll be in.'

Ronnie laughed.

'He's always in when it's daylight,' she said. She grinned at Jake. 'We call him the vampire.'

'Benjy the Vampire?' said Jake, laughing despite himself. 'It doesn't really have a terrifying ring to it.'

They walked north from Oxford Street, to the outer reaches of Regent's Park, and then crossed Marylebone Road, where luxury houses and flats gave way to street after street of council flats. Benjy, it seemed, lived on the third floor of one of the blocks, and as they walked along the balcony to the flat, Jake could hear music coming from inside — so loud it made the concrete beneath their feet vibrate.

'Don't his neighbours complain about the noise?' asked Jake.

Jez shook his head.

'That ain't from Benjy's,' he said. 'That's from his neighbours, some old gran and grandad couple.'

The trio walked past the flat with the thumping music, and arrived at the door of the next flat. Jez rang the bell. Jake was surprised that anyone inside the flat would be able to hear the sound of the bell with the deafening sound of drums'n'bass from the next flat, but Benjy obviously had his ears tuned in for it. He opened the door a crack and peered out suspiciously, and then opened it wider when he saw it was Jez and Ronnie.

'Yo!'

Jez gestured with his thumb at Jake.

'We got a refugee here,' he said. 'Needs some help.'

Benjy opened the door wider.

'Come on in,' he said.

With that, he went into one of the rooms off the hallway.

Jez and Ronnie ushered Jake in, then shut the door, but it didn't shut out the noise of the music from next door.

162

'Doesn't Benjy complain about the noise?' asked Jake.

'Well, officially this flat is empty,' said Jez. 'And if Benjy complained they'd find out he was, like, livin' here, and then they'd kick him out. And they'd also find out about everyone else who's living here, too, and kick them out.'

Jake frowned.

'Everybody else?' he asked. 'How many?'

'That depends on who's around at any one time,' said Ronnie.

'So you two live here?' asked Jake.

Jez shook his head.

'We don't live anywhere,' he said. 'We just stay with friends now and then.'

Jake looked at them. They seemed to be about fifteen.

'You're runaways,' he said, startled at the sudden realisation.

Ronnie looked at him angrily, and then turned to Jez.

'I told you it was a mistake helping him,' she said.

'No,' Jake assured them. 'You can trust me. I won't say anything.'

'You say that now, but what about when you get out of this flat?' demanded Ronnie. 'For all we know you go runnin' to the police!'

'That ain't likely, Ronnie,' pointed out Jez. 'He's on the run, remember.'

'Yeah, but he might try and cut a deal. Sell us out to get himself off the hook.'

In spite of himself, Jake couldn't help smiling at her accusation.

'Really, you don't need to worry,' he said. 'That is so not me!'

'Oh yeah?' demanded Ronnie, still angry. 'How we know? You, with your good clothes and the way you talk.' Angrily, she turned on Jez. 'Why we helpin' this fool again?' she demanded.

'Because I got a feelin' about him,' said Jez defensively. 'He's OK. He's just a guy in need of help. He's clean.'

Ronnie shook her head.

'You said that before, and look what happened. We nearly ended up back in the home . . .' Then she realised what she'd said and shut up abuptly, whirling back to glare defiantly at Jake.

They're runaways from a children's home, realised Jake.

'I won't say anything,' he said. 'I know what some of those places can be like. Children's homes. Foster homes.'

Jez hesitated, then shook his head.

'You don't know,' he grunted.

'Oh, but I do,' countered Jake.

Ronnie looked at him scornfully.

'Yeah, from things you read in the papers and see on the TV,' she snapped at him angrily. 'But that ain't the same as livin' it!'

'But I did live it,' said Jake quietly. 'I was raised in foster homes, some good, some bad, some I never even wish to think about ever again.'

Jez and Ronnie looked at Jake, astonished.

'You serious?' asked Jez.

Jake nodded.

'What happened?' asked Ronnie. 'You taken into care?'

'No,' said Jake. 'I never knew my parents. Never knew who they were. I was left on the doorstep of a police station with a note saying "Please look after him". They reckon I was about three months old.'

Jez and Ronnie stared at him, stunned expressions on their faces.

'So you know the system,' said Ronnie, awed.

'Yep,' said Jake.

'You never find out who your ma was?' asked Jez.

Jake shook his head.

'At first I never asked, I just got on with it. There were too many other things to worry about, like staying away from the bad kids in the home.'

'Tell us about it!' nodded Ronnie in fervent agreement.

'Then I got farmed out to foster homes.' He smiled

165

at a memory. 'There was one couple, they were really nice. Mr and Mrs Danvers. John and Mary. They were really good. Kind. They looked after me.'

'How old were you then?'

'Eleven,' said Jake.

'Why didn't you stay with them?' asked Ronnie.

'Maybe he did,' put in Jez.

'No,' said Jake sadly. 'They both died from cancer. Her first, then him. So I got taken away and sent to someone else.' His expression darkened. 'It's always worse when you've been somewhere good, and then it gets snatched away and you end up somewhere really bad. Anyway, I ended up back at the home, and then got sent out a few more times, and then back to the home, until I was sixteen, when I left.'

'That's what me and Ronnie gonna do,' nodded Jez. 'We got six months left till we sixteen, then we can be legal. Get proper papers and jobs an' everything. Till then, we got to keep our heads down and not get in any trouble.'

'It ain't easy out there, even being legit,' Jake told them.

'You did OK,' said Jez. 'Look at you, with your suit and a good job.'

'And on the run,' added Jake.

'So why is that?' demanded Ronnie.

'Hey, Ronnie, that ain't our business,' protested Jez.

'Yes it is,' said Ronnie. 'We spending our precious time with this guy, we puttin' ourselves on the line for him, we deserve to know why.'

'Yes, you do.' Jake nodded in agreement.

And so Jake told them. About the Order of Malichea. About Lauren. Gareth, Pierce Randall and the Watchers. Finding the book at Glastonbury. Robert being beaten nearly to death. When he'd finished, Jez and Ronnie were staring at him, dazed.

'This is just about *books*?' said Ronnie, disbelief in her tone.

'It's about what the books mean,' explained Jake. 'Money to some, power to others, the good of the whole world to people like me and Lauren.'

Ronnie shook her head.

'But it's still about *books*!' she repeated, incredulous.

'For which these people will kill,' Jake reminded her.

'Why ain't you got no friends can help you?' asked Jez. 'You say there's people on your side, like this reporter woman . . .'

'Michelle,' nodded Jake.

'Why don't you call her?' Jez asked.

'Because I daren't use my mobile,' said Jake. He explained about being able to be tracked by the signal from a mobile phone. Jez and Ronnie exchanged interested looks.

'Even when it's off?' asked Jez.

'Even when it's off,' confirmed Jake. 'I need to get hold of another phone.'

'No problem,' said Jez. 'What sort you want? One where you can get movies and games and stuff?'

'No, just one I can use to make phone calls.'

'No problem,' said Ronnie. 'We'll fix you up tomorrow. Jez knows a guy who does the best deals.'

'I just need a pay-as-you-go with a new number,' said Jake. 'One they don't know is me.'

'Leave it to me,' said Jez confidently. 'You got a cash card?'

Jake hesitated. Was this their way of getting his card off him to take his money. Then he remembered what they'd done for him already and felt guilty for even thinking that.

'Yes,' he said.

'OK. Right now, we'll stay here the night. Then first thing tomorrow you get some cash, then we'll get you a phone.'

Chapter 22

As night came, more and more people, most of them in their teens, came into the flat. The kitchen was in constant use, the microwave being especially busy. No one seemed to take much notice of Jake. A few times Jake noticed some of the kids murmuring to Jez or Ronnie as they cast a suspicious look in his direction, but whatever Jez or Ronnie said obviously quelled any suspicions about him.

All the time, the music from next door carried on. Then, on the stroke of ten o' clock, the music stopped. Or, rather, it was replaced by music that could barely be heard through the walls.

'They know the law,' explained Jez. 'Loud during the day, quiet at night. That way they don't get busted.'

'So they're really a law-abiding couple, Gran and Grandad next door,' said Jake.

Ronnie grinned.

'No,' she said. 'They just like annoyin' people. She grinned. 'We call it music wars.'

That night, Jake joined Jez and Ronnie in the smallest room in the flat, bunking down on sleeping bags laid out on the floor. It wasn't the most comfortable place that he had ever slept in, and he was aware that the flat was full of strangers, but he felt safer here than he had done for quite a while. He was pretty sure that Gareth's people, and Alex Munro's, hadn't traced him to here. Nor had anyone else.

Tomorrow, he'd get himself a new phone and call Michelle. Then he'd make contact with Lauren. He wouldn't be able to tell her all the things that had happened, especially what had happened to Robert, but he could at least reassure her that things were moving forward. That they were on the right lines.

Just before he fell asleep, his thoughts went to Robert in hospital, and the dreadful question: who had done that to him?

Next morning, Jake left the flat with Jez and Ronnie, and within a short while he'd got his new phone and £20 worth of credit. He looked at the small piece of equipment he held in his hand and felt a sense of relief. He was connected again. He could talk to people. He could even call Lauren, although his credit would likely just buy him a few seconds to New Zealand. No, the first person he'd call would be Michelle; he would arrange for her to set up the story about the book. He was just about to put in her number, when Jez stopped him, putting his hand over Jake's. Jez had a worried look on his face.

'I bin thinkin',' he said, frowning. 'What you said about them tracing you with your phone.'

'Yes, but that's why I've got this one,' said Jake. 'They don't know this number.'

'But they will do once you start using it,' said Jez. 'Ronnie said it to me just now.'

Jake looked questioningly at Ronnie.

'You make a call, that number gonna register, right?' she said. 'Say these people, these agents or whatever, are listening into whoever you might be callin'. Like this Michelle woman. Once you make that call and they listen and find out it's you, they got your number.'

Jake stared at her, stunned, then back at the phone in his hand.

'And you didn't think to tell me this *before* I bought this phone?' he said, angry.

'We didn't think of it before,' defended Jez.

'*You* didn't think of it *at all*,' pointed out Ronnie. 'If I hadn't said anythin', you'd be bein' grabbed by those men.'

Yes, that was a good point, thought Jake. And he should have thought of it. He slipped the phone into his pocket.

'Maybe you could call Michelle for me?' he asked hopefully.

'And have them chasin' me once they got *my* number?' demanded Jez indignantly. He shook his head. 'No way!'

Jake was frustrated. He'd been depending on talking to Michelle, and then getting the book to her. But there was still another way. He pulled out Michelle's business card. Yes, there were her email addresses: one at the magazine, one at home.

'Where's the nearest cybercafé?' he asked.

Fifteen minutes later, Jake was sitting at a computer sending Michelle a message.

I need to see you urgently, he typed. *Can't phone. I'll explain when we meet. When, and where?*

As he clicked 'send' he prayed that she would be at a computer somewhere, either at home or at her office, and would get his message, and respond quickly.

Jake then sent a message to Lauren: *Sorry I've been out of touch. Can't get to my flat at the moment, and can't phone. I'll explain later. But there's good news. Something has come up.*

He wondered if he was being too cryptic, and if Lauren would realise that 'something has come up' meant a book had been dug up. The problem was, if his message was too obvious, Gareth's spooks would spot it. But then, Gareth knew he had the book already.

He felt a surge of relief as the inbox displayed a reply from Michelle: *12 noon. The office*.

When he came out of the cybercafé, Jez and Ronnie were waiting for him, looking at him enquiringly.

'I got a meet set up with this reporter,' he told them. 'This'll soon be over.'

'You want us to come with you?' asked Jez. 'Watch your back?'

Jake shook his head.

'No,' he assured them. 'I should be OK now.'

'These people still after you,' Jez pointed out.

'I know,' said Jake, 'but I've got to do this on my own. You've done more than enough for me already,' he added gratefully.

He held out his hand and shook theirs.

'When this is all over I'll come and see you,' he said. 'I owe you big time.'

At twelve, Jake was in the reception foyer of *Qo* magazine in Villiers Street, anxiously scanning the crowd of workers as they left the building heading for the various sandwich bars and cafés for lunch. Finally, to his relief, he saw Michelle.

She came towards him, a look of annoyance on her face.

'Where have you been?' she demanded. 'I've been leaving messages for you on your voicemail!'

'It's a long story,' said Jake. 'And right now, it's not safe for me out in the open.'

'Yes, Robert told me about Andy,' said Michelle. She frowned. 'And where's Robert? When I couldn't get hold of you I tried him, but he's not answering either.'

'He was attacked,' said Jake. 'He's in a coma. He's got a fractured skull. And now they're looking for me.'

Michelle looked at him, horrified.

'Attacked?' she echoed.

'Like I said, it's a long story,' Jake told her. 'Is there anywhere here we can talk in private?'

Michelle thought it over, then said, 'The researcher's office should be free at the moment. We'll try there.'

They were in luck, the small glass-walled office was free.

'Right,' said Michelle when they had sat down. 'Let's hear it.'

As briefly as he could, Jake told her what had happened: the attack on him by Andy at the truck stop;

his escape; getting to his flat to find Andy watching it; going to Robert's house at Baron's Court and finding Robert badly beaten and unconscious; the phone calls from Gareth and Alex Munro; and being chased by, he assumed, Gareth's MI5 spooks; and getting rid of his phone and now hiding out.

Michelle heard him out, then said, 'We need to get the book out there into the public domain. That's the only way to stop this.'

Jake nodded. 'I agree,' he said.

'Good. Let me have the book and I'll get it opened in a lab, just like you said. Full hazard conditions, loads of photos, the lot.' She looked at her watch. 'I've got a lab all set up to do the tests. They're just over the river at Waterloo.'

'I haven't got it,' said Jake. 'I stashed it somewhere safe when I realised what was going on. But I can get it in an hour.'

Michelle nodded.

'OK, you get back here with the book. I'll prepare the lab, so they'll be expecting us.' Suddenly she beamed. 'This is going to be so good! This story's got everything! Murder, conspiracy, torture, religion, weird sciences . . . and it's all true! I'm going to make sure I get my own byline on this piece, and in big letters!'

'I'll just be glad to see it out there,' said Jake. And

Lauren back here with me, he added to himself. He got up and headed for the door. 'I'll see you in an hour.'

He stepped out of the offices into Villiers Street and headed towards Charing Cross station. Ten minutes on the Northern Line to Euston, ten minutes to get back, and the rest of the time waiting on platforms and at the Left Luggage office. In one hour, this would all be over. He turned to check for traffic as he stepped off the pavement, and a fist came out of nowhere and smashed him right in the face. He felt himself falling, dazed, his head filled with pain. Then he was being bundled inside the back of a car, his face pushed hard against the seat cover. He was aware of someone getting into the car beside him, the car door slamming, and then the car racing off.

Chapter 23

A gun was pushed into his face, the barrel pressing painfully into his cheek.

'Any funny business and you get a bullet in the leg,' said the man. 'We need you alive, but that don't mean we can't hurt you. Understood?'

Jake forced a nod. He felt sick.

The man sitting in the back of the car next to Jake lowered the gun and rested it on Jake's leg, pointing at his knee. He was broad-shouldered, the hand that held the gun big and powerful. Jake's head was still throbbing from the punch. From the force of the punch, and the man's bent and flattened nose and the scars around his eyes, Jake guessed he'd once been a boxer. He still had the power to hit hard.

The man in front of the car at the steering wheel was shorter and thinner. Not that Jake could see much of him, but he guessed that from the man's thin neck, and the way he sat low in the driver's seat.

'Put your head down,' ordered the Boxer.

'What?' asked Jake.

'Put your head down, face forward,' the man snapped, and he poked the end of the barrel of the gun warningly into the side of Jake's leg.

They don't want me to know where I'm going, thought Jake. He put his head down, twisting in the back seat so it touched his knees. The big fist that held the gun was now right by his eyes.

'What do you want?' asked Jake. 'I haven't got anything.'

'The book,' said the man with the gun. 'The one you found at . . .' He frowned. 'Where was it?'

'Glastonbury,' said the man at the front.

'Yeah. Glastonbury,' grunted the Boxer.

'I haven't got it,' said Jake.

'Then that's a pity,' said the driver. 'Because we're going to have to hurt you until you tell us where it is.'

After what seemed an eternity, the car finally stopped. Jake heard the driver's door open, and footsteps, and another door opening.

'OK. Out,' ordered the Boxer.

Jake sat up. He felt stiff all over from having held his twisted-up position in the back of the car. He opened the car door and got out. They were by a row of lock-up garages, one of which was open. Jake now saw that the other man was, indeed, short and thin. Shorty gestured at Jake.

'In,' he said.

The Boxer prodded Jake with the gun, and Jake walked into the garage. Shorty locked the car, then pulled down the garage door. It closed with an ominous click as it locked shut. The garage was lit by two over-head fluorescent lights. The central area was clear to allow a car in, but right now there was just a chair on its own in the middle of the garage.

Jake was reminded of the chair he'd woken up tied to in the timber yard in Holloway Yard. Had that been these same two men? Something told him no; apart from the chloroform, he hadn't been injured. These two were set on inflicting pain.

Shorty walked Jake to the chair, and began to tie him to it with ropes. The memory of Robert's body, battered, bruised and bleeding, tied to a chair in his living room, flashed in Jake's mind.

'You're the men who hurt Robert,' he blurted out.

'That's an allegation, that is,' said Shorty, pulling the ropes tight around Jake's wrists.

'He wouldn't tell us what we wanted to know,' grunted the Boxer.

'You fractured his skull!' said Jake angrily. 'You nearly killed him!'

'So, if you know that, ask yourself, how much do you want to be hurt?' asked Shorty, and he looked into Jake's face and gave a grin that sent a shiver of fear through him. The short man's smile was evil. The Boxer's the tough one, but Shorty likes inflicting pain, Jake realised.

When the punch came it was short but hard, smashing into Jake's face, catching him high on the head and rocking him back, the chair tilting with it. Pain filled Jake's brain. As the chair rocked forward, Shorty swung his other fist. As it connected, more pain surged through him. This time when the chair tilted, it carried on, and Jake found himself smashing into the concrete floor of the garage. The taste of blood filled his mouth, and he knew he was bleeding from his forehead, when he'd hit the ground hard as he toppled sideways, still tied to the chair.

'Want me to have a go?' asked the Boxer.

Jake looked up and saw Shorty shake his head. He was grinning, and Jake knew he was enjoying this.

'Nah,' he said. 'Anyway, that's just for starters, to let him know we mean business. Put him back up.'

The Boxer ambled over to Jake, reached under his arms and lifted him and the chair up as if they weighed nothing. He put Jake and the chair back down in the centre of the garage. Jake's head was throbbing painfully from the punches, and from where he'd fallen.

His forehead screamed with pain from grazing it on the concrete, and blood dripped down past his eyes and trickled from between his lips. He wondered if any of his teeth were loose.

Shorty grinned at Jake, then stepped away from him and gestured at the garage walls. Mechanic's tools of all sorts hung from hooks.

'When we were at your friend's house we had to improvise,' said Shorty, his cheerful tone making Jake feel even sicker to his stomach. 'But here, we've got everything we need: pliers, heavy-duty car batteries and jump leads, claw hammers, screwdrivers.' He smiled. 'And the beauty of it is we're away from the main road, so no one can hear you scream.'

He walked back and stood in front of Jake.

'So, what's it to be? You tell us where the book is or we start to take you apart. How much do you reckon you can take before you tell us?' He turned to the Boxer and asked, 'How long d'you reckon he'll hold out? Two fingernails? A broken arm?' He turned back to Jake, saying, 'I reckon you'll talk once we've fixed a car battery to a certain very sensitive part of your anatomy and sent a few serious charges through you. The skin burns from the inside, you know. There's that smell of roasted meat, and then the skin starts smouldering. Sometimes it even bursts into flames. It's the fat under the skin, so someone told me.'

181

He nodded. 'Yes, I reckon we'll start with the car battery.'

With that he walked over to the garage wall and loaded a car battery on to a trolley. He pushed the trolley to the chair. Then he took a pair of jump leads down from the wall. He snapped the metal clips at the end of the two wires as he walked back to Jake. He was smiling the whole time.

I can't do this, thought Jake. I'll tell them as soon as they start. It's not just a few seconds of pain, or even a few minutes, like in a dentist's chair. This will go on and on, for hours, maybe days, and at the end of it I'll be dead.

But I can't let them have the book. It's our only chance of getting Lauren back.

As Shorty began to connect the jump leads to the battery, Jake felt fear forcing the vomit to rise in his throat and knew he was going to throw up. I have to play for time! he thought. I have to stall them!

'It's in my flat!' he blurted out.

Shorty stopped and looked at him. He looked disappointed.

'What?' he asked.

'It's in my flat,' Jake repeated.

If I can get them to take me to my flat, I've got a chance of getting away from them, he thought. Here, in this torture chamber, I've got no chance.

Shorty shook his head.

'I don't believe you,' he said.

'I'll take you there and show you,' said Jake, his voice desperate.

Shorty and the Boxer exchanged looks.

'What do you reckon?' asked Shorty.

The Boxer shrugged.

'He could be telling the truth,' he said.

Shorty studied Jake, frowning thoughtfully.

'You could be lying,' he mused.

'It's in my flat!' insisted Jake, not knowing what else to say. 'In a bag on the top of my wardrobe.'

Shorty didn't move, nor did his thoughtful expression change as he looked at Jake. He knows I'm lying, thought Jake. He's going to torture me anyway. Finally, Shorty nodded.

'OK,' he said. 'I'll go and check it out.' Turning to the Boxer, he said, 'You stay here and keep an eye on him. I'll phone you when I get to his place.' Turning back to Jake, he asked: 'Keys?'

'In my pocket.'

Shorty rummaged around in Jake's pocket, and pulled out the two keys.

'My address is . . .' began Jake, but Shorty cut him off.

'We know where you live, stupid. That's where we started.' He pocketed the keys, and said warningly to

183

the Boxer, 'Don't let him try any funny business. If he does, shoot him in the leg, like you said.' To Jake, he said menacingly, 'If the book's not there, you are in for some very serious pain.'

With that, Shorty went to the garage door, opened it, stepped outside, and slammed it closed again. They heard the car engine start up.

The Boxer took the gun from his pocket and pointed it at Jake.

'A bullet in the leg is very, very painful,' he said threateningly. 'You have been warned.'

Chapter 24

Jake sat, tied to the chair, and watched the Boxer, waiting for any sign that he might have a chance to overpower him. Maybe if he came near enough he could trip him, topple him over, and kick him in the head, knocking him unconscious. But even as he said it to himself, Jake knew it was a fantasy. The Boxer stayed at a distance from Jake, sitting on an upturned crate, the gun held confidently in his big fist, his eyes fixed on Jake the whole time.

Jake had been relieved when he knew that Shorty was going to be the one going to his flat. In his mind, Shorty was the nasty one. He also seemed to be the cleverest of the pair. Left alone with the Boxer, Jake might have a chance. Left alone with Shorty, Jake knew he'd have no chance whatsoever. But the reality of the Boxer being left to guard him was that Jake had no chance of getting away from either of them. All he could do was sit and wait, and think about what would happen when Shorty discovered there was no book.

Jake and the Boxer had been sitting in the same positions for what Jake thought must have been an hour, when the Boxer's mobile rang.

'Yes?' said the Boxer. He listened, then turned to Jake. 'He says it's not there.'

'It is!' insisted Jake desperately, trying to think his way out of this. 'It's on top of the wardrobe in a white plastic shopping bag!'

The Boxer walked towards Jake, the phone in one hand, the gun in the other.

'He wants to talk to you,' he said. And he held the phone to Jake's ear.

'You lied!' hissed Shorty's angry voice. 'You sent me on a fool's errand! I'm going to take you apart bit by bit when I get back!'

'It's there!' shouted Jake desperately. 'I left it there when I got back from Glastonbury!' He paused, then added in a flash of inspiration: 'Someone must have taken it.'

'Who?' demanded Shorty.

'Anyone,' said Jake. 'Pierce Randall. The Watchers. MI5. Any one of all the people who are after it!'

There was a pause, then Shorty said, 'I'm going to have another look round. But if it ain't here, you're in serious trouble when I get back.'

The phone went dead. The Boxer put it back in his inside pocket.

'He doesn't like it when people try to play him for a mug,' he told Jake menacingly. Then he went back to the crate, and sat down again, his eyes and the gun on Jake.

It seemed all too soon to Jake when they heard the sound of the car pulling up outside and the garage door being lifted up. Shorty walked in, and closed the garage door shut behind him. He walked over to Jake and punched him hard in the face.

'No one plays me for a sucker and gets away with it!' He snarled. He punched Jake hard in the face again, and this time Jake felt blood pour down from his nostrils and tasted the salty liquid on his lips.

'It was there!' he managed to blurt out through the pain. 'Where I said it was. Someone must have taken it!'

'Who?' demanded Shorty angrily. 'Who else is after it? We were told if you hadn't got it, the only others who might know where it was were your pal, Robert George, and that reporter woman, Michelle; so we were to stake them out.'

'There's more than that,' said Jake. 'There's all those people I said: Pierce Randall. The Watchers. MI5.'

'What have MI5 got to do with it?' asked the Boxer, curious.

'He's lying,' snapped Shorty dismissively.

'The book's a government secret,' said Jake. 'Ask whoever's paying you, if you don't believe me. All of them are looking for the book, and all of them know I've got it.' He spat out a mouthful of blood and looked Shorty directly in the eyes. 'I thought you must be working for one of them.'

Shorty looked at Jake thoughtfully, and then moved away, taking out his mobile phone as he did so. He called up a number, and when it answered said, 'It ain't where he said it was. He reckons someone else took it. He's given us a few names of other outfits that he says are looking for it and he reckons one of them must have snaffled it.' Shorty then listened for a while, before answering: 'He could be lying, or it could be gone. What d'you want us to do?' He listened a bit more, before saying, 'OK.' Then he hung up his phone.

The Boxer looked at Shorty enquiringly.

'The pigs?' he asked.

Shorty nodded.

'Lucky old pigs,' he said, and grinned.

They untied Jake from the chair, and then tied his wrists together and took him outside, where they dumped him in the back seat of the car. Shorty got behind the wheel, and the Boxer slid into the passenger seat. He showed Jake the gun.

'Try any funny business and you'll get a bullet,' he said. 'And it won't be in the leg.'

'Yes.' Shorty nodded. 'For whatever reason, our boss seems to think you might be telling the truth. Which means you're no use to him any more. So you're for the chop.'

The way that Shorty said the words in such a casual way made Jake go cold as ice. They're going to kill me! They're going to take me somewhere and kill me! But, why not do it here?

Shorty started the car engine and turned to look back at Jake.

'Just in case you get any fancy thoughts about jumping out, the back doors are fitted with child-proof locks. All very safe.'

They're hoping I'll talk, thought Jake. That's why they're not killing me straight away. They're going to drive around and hope I'll crack and tell them where the book is. I've still got a chance.

But Shorty's next words, as the car moved off along an alleyway to join the main stream of traffic, crushed that hope.

'In case you think this is just to frighten you into telling us where the book is, you can forget it,' said Shorty. 'Our boss believes you. Personally, I don't. But then, that's just me. So he says we're to get rid of you.

189

'Now, I expect you're wondering why we didn't just kill you back in the garage? Well, the fact is, a dead body has to be disposed of, and that ain't as simple as people think, especially in a crowded city like London. So we've got an arrangement with a friend of ours out in the country who's got a pig farm. Pigs are great, they'll eat anything.'

'Especially if it's shredded up into small bits,' added the Boxer.

'And luckily our friend has got a really big industrial shredder at his farm,' said Shorty.

'It shreds Christmas trees.' He grinned. 'Guess what it can do to you.'

They are going to kill me, Jake realised. This wasn't just a bluff. He also realised that even if he had told them where the book was, they would have killed him, anyway. He'd seen their faces, he could identify them.

The car had left the city now and was out in the suburbs, heading towards woodland and open fields. The garage must have been right at the very east end of London, close to Essex.

There has to be a way to stop this happening, thought Jake. I'm going to die, anyway, if I don't try something. He looked at the road ahead, at the vehicles hurtling towards them on the other side of the road, then past them. No barriers, just fast traffic in two directions.

No crash barriers at the sides of the road either, just countryside: woodlands on this side of the road.

Jake fought to keep down the feeling of panic rising in him. Attack them. That's the only way. Make the car crash. They might kill me as I try, but at least I'll have a chance. And, if I get killed in the car crash, I'll take them with me.

He tensed himself, took a deep breath, and suddenly he jerked forward, his tied hands raised up, and then dropped them down over Shorty's head. He pulled back hard, the rope biting across the front of Shorty's throat. Taken by surprise, Shorty let go of the steering wheel and reached up to his neck, his hands clawing at the rope as Jake pulled back even harder, choking him.

The Boxer turned, a horrified look on his face, but he was too late.

The whole action had taken barely a second, but already the car was out of control, veering to the left, straight for the trees at the side of the road.

SMASH!!

The car hit a tree head-on, and as it did so the air bags at the front exploded, smothering the two men in the front seats.

Jake ripped his tied hands upwards, tearing them across Shorty's face.

The impact of the collision had sprung all the car doors open, and Jake scrambled out. He saw that the

191

Boxer's gun had fallen from his hand and was lying on the ground near the open door. The Boxer was struggling with the air bag, trying to get clear of it.

Jake scooped up the gun and put it against the Boxer's knee. He didn't allow himself to think, he just pulled the trigger. The Boxer screamed as the bullet tore into his leg, shattering his knee.

Jake pointed the gun across the Boxer in the direction of Shorty. Shorty didn't move, but Jake heard him groaning. He was still alive.

I can't take the chance of him chasing me, thought Jake. If he gets out of this, he'll kill me. His finger began to tighten on the trigger, but then he stopped. This will be murder, he thought. I can't do it.

Instead, Jake thrust his hands into the Boxer's jacket pocket and pulled out the man's mobile phone. He was aware of cars pulling to a halt on the road, as other drivers stopped to offer assistance.

Jake ran, heading into the wooded area, pushing the gun and the phone into his pockets as he ran. He didn't know how deep the wood was. All he knew was that it would give him cover.

Chapter 25

Jake ran through the woods, ducking under low-hanging branches, sharp brambles tearing at his clothes, until he reached a place where there was a rough track and the foliage and undergrowth was clearer. Running was made even more difficult with his hands tied together.

He dropped to the ground, dragging himself into the cover afforded by bushes growing around the base of a large old tree. His heart was beating so fast he thought it would burst. I've got to get these ropes off, he told himself. He set to work with his teeth, pulling at the knots, and finally he had separated the rope that tied him enough to wriggle his wrists free.

The gun felt heavy in his pocket. I have to get rid of it, he thought. It's evidence against me. But if he dumped it here, it would certainly be found once the police started searching these woods. Because that was one thing for sure: the police would search this area once they realised one of the men in the crashed car had been shot. He couldn't stay here for long.

He pushed himself up from the dry earth and stood, listening. He could hear voices coming from the direction he'd run from. Was it the police already? He broke into a sprint, putting as much distance between him and the scene of the crash as he could. How big was this wood? Where was it? He guessed they had left London from the north-west, and if that was the case that would mean they were somewhere in Essex. Was this Epping Forest? If so, it went on for miles and miles, and he could easily get lost, and be picked up by the police when they began searching.

He heard traffic noises ahead of him, and he stopped. Cautiously, he moved forward, scanning the area ahead of him through the trees. He could see the fronts of houses, and hear the sounds of a road. He kept moving, and saw that he was coming towards what seemed to be a housing estate: neat semi-detached houses and bungalows on the other side of a quiet road bordering the wood.

He crossed the road to the pavement on the other side, and then began walking blind, hoping that he was heading in the right direction and not into a dead-end. There didn't seem to be any people around. Jake guessed this was commuter land, with most people out at work. He wondered whether to go up and knock on a door and ask where he was, but realised that such an action would only arouse suspicion; and whoever he asked would surely be on the phone to the police as soon as they shut the door on him.

He came to a road sign, telling him that he was walking along Elm Way; then another at a turning saying that this one was called Oak Avenue. The next street was Willow Path. Obviously part of the original woods had been bought up by a developer and turned into this housing estate.

Suddenly, as if it was a mirage, he saw a black London cab standing outside one of the houses. Someone was just paying off the driver. Jake saw the cab indicating to move off, and he ran out into the road, waving an arm to call the taxi to a halt. The cab driver looked at Jake and grinned.

'Well, this must be my lucky day,' he said. 'There was I thinking I'd have to drive back empty from the middle of nowhere.'

'Where are we?' asked Jake.

The driver looked at Jake suspiciously.

'You don't know where you are?' He peered closer at Jake, and the expression of suspicion on his face deepened as he took in the bruises on Jake's face, and his crumpled and stained clothes.

'I came here in my mate's car,' lied Jake. 'He brought me here, and now he's gone off, leaving me stranded.'

'Why?' asked the driver, still suspicious.

Jake sighed.

'We had a row,' he said. He gave a rueful smile. 'Long story.'

The driver looked at Jake thoughtfully, then asked: 'Is that why you look in such a state?'

Jake nodded.

''Fraid so,' he said.

The driver shook his head.

'It's none of my business, but I'd be careful who your mates are,' he said. 'Anyway, you're in Chigwell.'

Chigwell, thought Jake. Essex. On the outskirts of north-east London.

'OK,' said Jake. Quickly, he considered his options. He could get an underground train from Chigwell, but it could take time. He could ask the taxi to take him back into central London, but the streets would be gridlocked with traffic, even in the bus and taxi lanes; they always were. He'd be going nowhere. And then it suddenly hit him where he wanted to go. A place he hadn't been for a long time. Too long.

196

'D'you know the River Lea at Lea Bridge Road?' he asked.

The driver looked almost offended.

'I ought to, I was born near there,' he said. 'Right by Hackney Marshes. I played football on the marshes every Sunday.'

'That's where I want to go,' said Jake.

As the driver looked again at Jake's battered and crumpled state, his suspicious expression returned. 'You got money to pay for it?' he asked warily.

'Yes,' said Jake, and he took out his wallet and showed the driver the notes inside. The driver grinned.

'Jump in,' he said.

The taxi made its way through the maze that was the estate, and finally joined the main road back towards London. As they headed down the wide road, they saw police cars and an ambulance by the side of the road on the other side. The crashed car was still there, half off the road, its front buried among bushes and trees.

'Hello, an accident!' said the cab driver.

'Yes,' said Jake.

The driver shook his head.

'Too many mad people on the road,' he said. 'Give someone a driving licence and it's like giving them a gun. Half of them don't know how to drive a car properly, or think they know everything. And show them

197

a bit of open road and they think they're at Brands Hatch!' He shook his head. 'Speeding, I bet! Then they lose control.' He sighed. 'People like that shouldn't be allowed behind a wheel!'

Chapter 26

Jake sat on a tree stump on the towpath by the side of the River Lea looking at the houseboats moored along the bank. He remembered when he used to come here as a boy on Sunday mornings with John Danvers, while Mary Danvers prepared the Sunday roast. Just like the sort of family you saw on TV or read about in magazines. Jake had never known a family like that before. All the families he had encountered as a child were dysfunctional; the foster parents he was sent to live with, the families of the other kids at the different schools he went to. When he'd first gone to live with the Danvers, he was suspicious of them. No one could be that nice, not in his experience. But they were.

John Danvers was a car mechanic. Mary Danvers was a teaching assistant at a primary school. They lived in a neat two-bedroomed terraced house in Leyton. Jake was eleven years old when he went to live with them, and he spent the first three months just watching and waiting for some sort of nastiness to show beneath the surface. But there had been no nastiness; and Jake realised that with John and Mary Danvers it was a case of 'what you see is what you get'. They were a kind, loving couple who wanted to give a home to a child to make their family complete.

Jake remembered how he and John had walked along this towpath, pointing out the differences between the houseboats. 'Me and Mary often thought of living on a boat,' John told him. 'It's so quiet and peaceful here, on the water. Away from the noise and dirt of the streets and the roads.'

And it was still, Jake reflected.

He'd come here because he needed this time to sit and recover himself; and this was his special place. His sanctuary.

Not that he'd thought of it that way before. When Mary had discovered that she had cancer, everything had been thrown into turmoil. By then, Jake had been living with them for just over a year. Three months after Mary was diagnosed, she was dead.

Her death had destroyed John. Jake had done his best to help him, insisting that they went for their regular walk along this towpath, looking at the boats, and listening to John talking about Mary.

And then John had fallen ill, and also been diagnosed with cancer.

The childcare authorities had moved in, and before Jake had time to realise what was happening, John was in hospital, and Jake was back in the children's home.

Jake asked to go and visit John in hospital, but the authorities decided it wouldn't be right for Jake to visit John in his condition; that it would be too distressing for him. So Jake had run away and tried to get into the hospital to see John, but he'd been caught and returned to the children's home.

The next thing he knew, John had died, and Jake hadn't had a chance to see him and tell him how much he and Mary had meant to him. Because of that, Jake was even angrier at the authorities. He'd had to find private places where he could cry his grief for John and Mary without anyone seeing him.

Never again, he'd told himself. Never again will I let myself get so attached to anyone.

And that had been how it was until he'd met Lauren, and fallen in love with her. All he wanted to do now was get Lauren back. Which meant getting the book to the lab so Michelle could verify it, and publish her article.

He took out the phone he'd taken from the thugs, and dialled Michelle's number. She answered straight away.

'It's Jake,' he said.

'Where have you been?!' demanded Michelle, not even trying to disguise the anger in her voice. 'I've got everything set up! You promised you'd be here with the book!'

'I got held up,' said Jake.

There was a pause, and Jake was sure that Michelle had just realised that something bad must have happened to him.

'Serious?' she asked.

'Very serious,' confirmed Jake.

'OK,' she said. 'The thing is, you're ready now, right?'

'Yes,' said Jake. 'Only the last time I came to your office I got grabbed. I don't know who else may be watching there.'

'So we need to meet up somewhere else.'

'Yes, but I'm pretty sure this conversation is being listened to, so we can't say where.'

There was a pause, then Michelle said: 'Where we first met.'

Of course, realised Jake: the timber yard where Michelle had found him.

'OK,' he said.

'How soon can you be there?' asked Michelle.

Jake thought it over. Getting to Euston, collecting the book, then out to Holloway Road and the timber yard would take about an hour, providing nothing went

202

wrong again. But something was always going wrong. People were still out there, looking for him. People who would kill him. He needed help. He needed someone to watch his back.

'I'll call you,' he said.

As he stood up, the gun in his pocket banged against his side.

I don't need this, he thought. I'm not a killer. If I carry this, it could go wrong for me. I'm the one who could end up being shot.

He walked over to the edge of the towpath and looked down into the dark swirling waters. Even with all the clean-up of London's rivers that had been going on, here the water was so thick with sludge and silt, and muck from the boats, it was like soup. He looked around to make sure that no one was watching, then lifted the gun from his pocket and tossed it into the water.

OK, he told himself. Time to play the final card. But first, I need to get me some back-up.

Chapter 27

Jake stood on the balcony outside Benjy's flat. The music from next door was still pounding, although not as loudly as it had been the last time Jake had been here. He pressed the doorbell. After what seemed like ages, the door opened a crack and an eye peered out. Then the door opened a bit wider and Benjy looked out enquiringly at Jake. Jake noticed the security chain stayed in place.

'Hi,' said Jake, and he smiled.

'You're the guy who was here with Jez and Ronnie,' said Benjy warily.

'Right.' Jake nodded. 'Are they here?'

Benjy looked at him in surprise.

'Why would they be here?' he asked. 'They don't live here.' He grinned. 'They don't live anywhere. They fly by night.'

'Yes, well, is it possible for you to get in touch with them for me?'

Benjy regarded Jake suspiciously.

'Why would I do that?' he asked.

'Because I need to talk to them urgently.'

The look of suspicion remained on Benjy's face.

'You're accusing them of something?' he demanded.

Jake stared at him, indignant.

'No!' he said firmly. 'Why would I do that? They saved me! I owe them!'

Benjy stayed studying Jake, the suspicious look still on his face, then he said, 'Stay there.' With that he went into the flat and shut the door.

Jake looked around the balcony nervously. He didn't like staying exposed in one place for too long. After what seemed like an eternity, the door opened again and Benjy held out a mobile phone.

'Jez wants to talk to you,' he said.

Jake took the phone.

'Jez,' he said, relieved.

'You gotta be in trouble, Jake,' said Jez.

'I am,' admitted Jake.

'Get in the flat. I'll be along.'

With that, the phone went dead.

Jake handed the phone back to Benjy.

'He said . . .' he began.

'I heard,' said Benjy. He held the door open. 'You better come in.'

He let Jake in, and pointed to the kitchen.

'Make yourself at home,' he said. 'Only, you eat anything, put some money in the jar by the fridge. OK?'

'OK. Thanks.'

But Benjy had already gone into his room, and shut the door.

Jez arrived half an hour later. He took a look at Jake's bruised face and let out a low whistle.

'Someone messed you up,' he observed.

'Yep,' said Jake. 'They were going to kill me, but luckily I got away.'

Jez studied Jake, and Jake knew he was weighing up whether to ask him for details.

Instead, Jez said, 'I told you you should've had back-up.'

'You were right,' admitted Jake.

'So now, what's happening?'

'I need to pick up the book and get it to a lab so it can be tested,' said Jake. 'The book's in the Left Luggage office at Euston Station. The problem is, everyone who's after it seems to know what I'm about to do next.'

'If it's MI5 and them, they'll be using them CCTV cameras they got,' said Jez. 'They're all over every main station.'

206

Jake reflected that Jez was right.

'In which case they'll know I was at Euston, and maybe picked up that I left the book there in a rucksack.'

'And you're thinking they might have someone waiting there for you,' said Jez.

'Yes. My guess is it won't be a big stake-out, just one or two people at most, watching out for me; but when they see me, they'll give a call.'

Jez remained thoughtful.

'Where you got to get this book to?'

'A timber yard off Holloway Road,' said Jake.

'A timber yard?' echoed Jez in surprise.

'That's where I'm meeting the person who's going to take it to the lab.'

Jez was silent for a bit longer, then finally he nodded.

'OK,' he said. 'Here's what you do. Do you know the Ibis Hotel beside Euston?'

'No,' said Jake, 'but I can find it.'

'On the corner of Drummond Street and Cardington Street. Right opposite the western side entrance to Euston. You can't miss it. Go in there and wait in the reception area. There's tables and chairs and stuff, so you'll be OK. You'll just be someone waiting.'

'And then what?' asked Jake.

Jez thought it over.

'Give me two hours,' he said. 'Then things will happen.'

'What things?' asked Jake.

Jez smiled.

'That depends what I can fix up in the next two hours,' he said.

Chapter 28

Jake sat in the reception area of the Ibis Hotel, his eyes fixed on the glass double doors of the entrance. He'd been sitting here for half an hour, and so far there had been no sign of anyone he recognised from the flat. No Jez, no Benjy, no Ronnie, no one. Luckily, the reception area was full of other people waiting, most sitting with a tea or a coffee, or a newspaper, and all scanning every new face that appeared in case it was the person they were waiting for. Jake knew the bruises on his face made him conspicuous, but he hoped they'd help to make sure that people gave him a wide berth. No one wanted to get too close to someone whose face was marked by cuts and bruises. Luckily, he'd been able to damp his clothes down using the basins in the hotel toilet and get some of the stains off them.

He wondered what Jez was planning. Jake was sure that Euston would be watched, people waiting there for Jake to appear and collect the rucksack from the Left Luggage office. The big question was: by who? Gareth's MI5 spooks? Pierce Randall's people? Or the ones who'd sent those two thugs to find him and torture him, the ones who'd attacked Robert and left him near to death? Jake shuddered.

Suddenly he sat up, alert. The small figure of Ronnie had just walked into the entrance.

Jake stood up as she approached.

'OK,' she said. 'We're go.' And she held out something to Jake. At first he couldn't work out what it was, then he realised it was a crash helmet.

'What's this for?' he asked.

'In case you need it,' she said. 'The way people keep bashing you up, you need some protection.'

Jake shook his head.

'I'm not wearing this,' he said. 'I'll look ridiculous!'

'Take it,' she ordered, her voice taking no refusal.

'No,' said Jake. 'I'm not putting that on. I'd feel like a dork.'

Ronnie hissed at him: 'Listen. Jez says you gotta take it. And I ain't walkin' around any more holdin' it! I felt stupid enough walkin' around bringin' it here!' She thrust it at him. 'You don't wanna wear it, fine. But you carry it! And don't lose it. It cost money.'

Jake took the crash helmet from her. She gestured

towards the hotel entrance. 'Come on, time to go. Look sharp.'

'Where's Jez?' asked Jake.

Ronnie held up a mobile phone.

'He's just a call away,' she said.

Jake wasn't reassured.

'No offence, Ronnie, but these are tough people we're dealing with.'

'You sayin' I ain't tough?' demanded Ronnie, put out.

'No, no,' Jake assured her. 'You're one of the toughest people I've met, but these guys — or, at least, the ones I've met so far — are tough and nasty. They could be armed.'

Ronnie shrugged.

'We'll cross that road when we come to it,' she said.

'Bridge,' said Jake automatically.

Ronnie frowned.

'What?' she asked.

'The phrase is "We'll cross that bridge when we come to it" . . .'

Ronnie stared at him, incredulous.

'People are out there lookin' to kill you and torture you, and you hung up on the right and wrong *word*?' She shook her head. 'No wonder you always in so much trouble, you worry too much about the wrong things.'

She headed out of the Ibis, with Jake following her. At the kerb, she stopped and looked pointedly at Jake.

'We've come to a *road*. We're gonna cross it. That all right with you?'

'Fine.' Jake nodded, feeling sheepish.

They crossed the road and went into the side entrance of the station. All the time, Jake's eyes were darting left and right, scanning the crowds, trying to identify would-be attackers. But it was impossible to spot if anyone was watching for him, or paying particular attention to the Left Luggage office; the concourse was crowded with people waiting for trains; and the shops around the main concourse, and right up to the Left Luggage office, were filled with a constant traffic of people getting supplies for their journeys: newspapers, sandwiches, drinks.

As they neared the Left Luggage office, with its open counter and hundreds of items of luggage stacked on shelves behind, Ronnie ordered him, 'OK, put the helmet on.'

'What?' asked Jake, puzzled. 'Why?'

In answer, Ronnie held up her mobile phone. 'Because Jez says so,' she told him.

Jake frowned. He could only think that Jez wanted to protect him in case anyone attacked him and tried hitting him over the head. He thought wearing a crash helmet was a bit extreme, but then he remembered Robert's fractured skull.

'OK,' he said, and he pulled on the helmet.

'Good,' said Ronnie. 'Let's go get the thing.'

They arrived at the large open counter of the Left Luggage office and Jake pulled out his ticket and handed it over. The clerk examined it, then told him how much was due. Jake paid, and the clerk went to the rows of shelves, rummaged through them, and reappeared with the rucksack. As Jake took hold of it, he felt sick with apprehension. He had the book, but who was watching and waiting for him? There had to be someone, he was sure. Were they armed? Would they gun him down, here, in public? Yes, he had no doubt they would, if it meant them getting their hands on the book.

As Jake and Ronnie turned away from the counter, they came face to face with a man and a woman, both dressed in plain smart clothes. MI5? Special Branch? They had that air about them, hard, ruthless, determined.

'Police. We'll take that bag, please,' said the man.

'Oh no you don't!' screeched Ronnie. Suddenly she yelled out, 'Help! Kidnappers!'

At Ronnie's ear-splitting shout, the man and the woman looked bewildered and glanced around, as passengers stopped and looked towards them.

Ronnie swung her foot back and kicked the man hard on the shin, and he yelled out in pain and hopped backwards. The woman had recovered and was reaching for the rucksack held in Jake's hand, but Ronnie grabbed her arm and sank her teeth into the woman's wrist. The woman yelled and hit out at Ronnie, but Ronnie ducked.

There was a loud roar of a motorbike engine right by them, and Jake suddenly saw a small trials motorbike had screeched past them and skidded to a halt.

'Jump on!' yelled the rider.

It was Jez.

Suddenly, he realised why Ronnie had given him the crash helmet. He saw the woman throw Ronnie to the ground and leap at him, her fingers outstretched again for the rucksack. Jake dodged to one side, and then jumped on the back of the bike. Jez stood up on the footrests, allowing Jake to plonk himself down on the seat. Jake barely had time to get a grip on the back of the bike, when Jez slammed it into gear and it tore away, heading for the main concourse.

By now, uniformed police officers and Transport Police, alerted by the sound of the motorbike, had appeared and were giving chase, spreading out across the concourse to intercept the bike. Their attempts were made harder by the mass of passengers, most with piles of luggage around them, but they also presented Jez and the bike with obstacles. Not that Jez seemed bothered, he revved and raced the machine, weaving in and out of the people, skidding as they leapt towards him, and then righting it again. Jake clung on grimly as they jumped and skidded left and right. Jez was making for the open double doors of the station that led to the outside piazza, and the flight of steps down to the main road.

Jake saw that five policemen had planted themselves in a line directly blocking off their escape route, in front of the open double doors. They held batons, and one of them looked to be armed and was taking a gun from a holster. There was no way the bike could squeeze past them!

Quickly, Jez veered the bike to the left. As he did so, the five policemen moved swiftly to form a line and try to block the bike's escape. Jake expected Jez to turn and find another route to get away, but instead Jez opened the throttle and hurtled the bike directly at the policemen, aiming at the already closing gap between two of them. One of the policemen leapt out of the way of the fast-approaching bike, but the other swung his baton at them. Jake saw the baton bounce off Jez's helmet, and then felt it hit the visor of his own, jerking him backwards. Jake clung on grimly, and felt the surge of the bike as it raced forward, heading for the large glass doors to the outside.

As they accelerated away from the police, Jake was worried that the automatic opening mechanism had been shut off, because the doors stayed shut and for a second he thought they were going to crash into the thick glass. Then, the doors opened and Jez was racing across the concrete towards a flight of steps. There was a roar as the bike left the ground, and once again they were flying through the air. The wheels hit the pavement. The bike bounced, and then Jez had turned it into the roadway, veering between the oncoming traffic.

They were away!

Chapter 29

Jez raced along the back streets and alleyways, along narrow rat runs where no car could follow, until they were well over a mile away from Euston station, before he pulled the bike to a halt.

'You get it?' he demanded of Jake.

Jake felt barely able to speak. The experience of clinging tightly to the bike as it had soared through the air, then crashed down to the hard concrete, had been one of the most terrifying experiences of his life.

No, he realised. His most terrifying experience had been the car ride with the men who had been going to kill him. But this bike ride had still left him shaking.

'Yes,' he managed to croak, and he held up the rucksack, which he'd been gripping so tightly his fingers seemed stuck to the straps.

'OK,' said Jez. 'Time to phone your journalist friend and tell her to get to the place. Tell her twenty minutes.' He grinned. 'I'm going to do back lanes and walkways the whole way, so we don't get picked up. So you put that rucksack on properly. We don't want it falling off, not after all the trouble we've been through.'

Jake nodded and pulled the rucksack on to his back. Then he phoned Michelle, though he had trouble tapping out her number, his fingers were still shaking so much.

'Yes?' she said.

'Where we said. In twenty minutes.'

'It might take me longer. Traffic.'

'As soon as you can,' said Jake. 'And when we've finished this call, disconnect your phone. Take out the batteries and the SIM card.'

'Why?' asked Michelle.

'Because they might track you using the signal.'

He hung up. Then, just in case his trackers had been able to pinpoint his position from the mobile he was using, he did the same as he'd advised Michelle: took out the battery and the SIM card and dropped his dismantled phone in his pocket.

'OK,' he told Jez. 'I'm ready.'

They pulled up outside the timber yard twenty-five minutes later, because of the number of detours that

Jez had taken to throw off any possible followers. As Jake got off the bike, he wobbled; and only then did he realise just how much tension had been in his legs and arms as he held on during the ride. As he stood, taking off the crash helmet and recovering, he heard the sound of a car pull up, and automatically swung round towards it, expecting it to be trouble — maybe Gareth's spooks. But it was Michelle.

'This your lift?' asked Jez.

'Yes.' Jake nodded.

'OK,' said Jez. 'You gonna be OK now?'

'I should be,' said Jake.

Jez smiled.

'Good,' he said.

'Listen,' said Jake awkwardly, 'I have to do something for you, pay you back in some way.'

'Sure.' Jez grinned. 'You get to be a millionaire, you come and find me. Till then, you stay safe, and get that woman of yours back home.'

Jake looked at him, overwhelmed with emotion. This fifteen-year-old, who he didn't know and had no ties of any sort to, had put himself in serious danger for him. And now he was just disappearing from Jake's life.

'I owe you, Jez,' he said. 'You and Ronnie.'

'Our paths will cross, and when they do, you can help us out, if we need it,' said Jez. 'That's the way the world is: we help one another out. We pass on the good thing. We do you a turn, you find someone else in trouble and you do them a turn.'

Jake smiled at him.

'Maybe Ronnie's right, maybe you've been hanging around them Hare Krishna people too much,' he said with a smile.

'Peace and love and looking after people who need help,' said Jez. 'It ain't no bad thing.' He looked towards Michelle, who had opened the door of her car and was waiting. 'Better go and do the last move, Jake.'

'Yes.' Jake reached out his hand, and shook Jez's. 'I'll pay you back someday, I promise,' he said.

'Sure you will.' Jez smiled. 'I know that.'

Then Jez slipped the bike into gear, and raced away. Jake watched him go then he walked to Michelle's car.

'You got it?' she asked.

'I got it.' Jake nodded.

'OK,' said Michelle, her eyes brightening with excitement. 'Let's get to the lab!'

Chapter 30

The lab was in a building that looked impressively high-tech from the outside. Michelle parked in the enclosed car park. Inside the building, once they'd passed through security, there were rows of corridors that appeared to house many labs, all with red lights on outside the doors, and signs outside each warning: 'No entry'. Jake followed Michelle to the lift, which they caught to the third floor. There seemed to be very few people about, and those that were wore white lab coats and hurried past them unsmiling and not making eye contact.

'This is our lab,' said Michelle, pointing to the number 23 by one of the doors. She took out a plastic card and ran it through the security decoder beside the door. There was a buzzing sound, then the door swung open. A young female lab technician in a white coat was waiting for them in a small entrance lobby.

'Ms Faure?' she asked.

Michelle nodded. 'And this is Jake Wells,' she said, gesturing at Jake.

Jake gave the young woman a smile, but it wasn't returned.

'Lucy Waning,' said the young woman. She held out her hand. 'You have the item?'

Jake took out the plastic bag and handed it to her.

'Be careful,' he warned her. 'The last time one of these was opened, there were spores inside it which infected the person who opened it.'

'That's why we are using a bio-hazard case,' said Waning. 'If there are any contaminents inside here, they'll be detected.' She indicated a side door marked 'Gallery'. 'If you go in there you'll be in the observation gallery, and you can watch what's happening.'

'Do we need to wear hazard suits, or whatever you call them?' asked Jake.

Waning shook her head.

'Not at this stage,' she said. 'And, hopefully, not at all. Inside the observation gallery you'll find monitors, so you'll be able to follow everything that I do as there are high-definition CCTV cameras aimed at the bio-hazard case from different angles which pick up everything. If you have any questions, or I want to ask you something during the procedure, the speakers and microphones inside the gallery will be switched on the whole time. Do you have any questions?'

Jake and Michelle exchanged questioning glances, then both shook their heads.

'No,' said Michelle. 'Everything seems to be covered.'

'Then I'll go and prepare and we can begin,' said Waning.

With that, she left the small lobby through a door marked 'Strictly no entry'. Jake followed Michelle through the door marked 'Gallery'.

As Waning had said, they were faced with banks of monitors, speakers built into the walls, and there were three microphones dangling down from the ceiling. The observation gallery was dimly lit. As well as being able to see everything via the monitors, one wall was completely glass and looked down on to a laboratory. They watched as Lucy Waning came into the laboratory. Now, she was wearing a hazard suit, complete with a large helmet with a visor at the front, with tubes and wires dangling from the front of the suit and the helmet. Jake thought she looked like an astronaut prepared for a space walk. In her hand she carried the plastic bag with the book in.

She went to a large glass case in the centre of the lab, lifted the lid, and placed the package inside. She shut the lid, and then clicked various switches to make sure it was sealed shut. Lights came on around the glass case.

'Those lights confirm the case is now sealed and airtight,' came Waning's voice over the speakers.

Waning then connected the ends of the different tubes and wires dangling from her suit and helmet to points at the base of the glass case.

'I am now connected to the unit,' said Waning. 'Everything I do will be recorded. If any hazard of any sort is detected, the units on the display above me will show the kind of hazard present, and the action the unit takes to neutralise it. Can you see the displays?'

Jake and Michelle looked at the top row of screens, which showed the sort of displays one saw in hospital emergency wards: lights pulsing, lines going up and down as they monitored everything inside the glass case.

'Yes,' said Jake.

Waning pushed her hands into a pair of gloves that were fixed to the case with airtight rubber seals, and set to work. As she removed the black leather case from inside the plastic bag, Jake felt his heart skip a beat of concern, wondering if the outside of the ancient leather had been contaminated. If so, then he would surely be affected in some way. But the various displays registered nothing alarming, just kept up a low beeping while the lines on the screens remained constant.

Waning pushed the bag to one side, and set the ancient black leather case in the centre of the base of the glass case.

'No contamination detected on or in the outer bag in which the object was delivered,' her unemotional voice said. 'No contamination detected on the exterior surfaces of object.' Jake and Michelle turned to the monitors and saw the black leather package magnified on the screens. 'The object appears to be made of leather treated with a preservative. Further tests will need to be carried out to identify the constituents of this preservative. The object is rectangular in shape, consistent with casing that may contain a small book of some sort. The surface is embossed with a symbol: a Roman letter "M" with what appears to be a snake of some sort intertwined in that letter.'

Yes, thought Jake, silently urging Waning to go faster and open the case. It's the Order of Malichea. We know that. Just get on and open it and find out what we've got.

'There are Roman numerals embossed on the material,' came Waning's flat and unemotional tones. 'DLVII. This translates as 557.'

Five hundred and fifty-seven! thought Jake excitedly. Then there really were hundreds of books out there, hidden like this one had been.

'I am going to open the outer casing,' said Waning. 'It appears to be closed by a simple slip knot of two leather strips.'

Jake watched, transfixed, as Waning's gloved fingers took hold of the ends of the leather strips that formed the small slip knot, and began to gently prise at them. After over five hundred years of being buried in soil, Jake wondered if they would be supple enough to be untied, or would they simply crack? Either way, the excitement and expectation in him at what was about to be revealed almost stopped him from breathing. He and Michelle watched in rapt silence as — in magnified close-up — Waning's gloved fingers teased and pulled at the knotted leather. There was obviously resistance.

'I am now using a small tool to aid undoing the knot,' announced Waning, and they watched as she took a small metal probe, rather like a small screwdriver, and used it to prise the strands of leather apart. Finally, the knot was undone.

'I am now opening the outer casing,' said Waning.

With that she carefully peeled back the old leather flaps of the protective casing, to reveal a small book inside. The covers and binding of the book appeared to be green. Waning slid the opened black leather casing from beneath the book, and pushed it to one side. There was now just the small green book in the centre of the glass case.

'I am opening the cover of the book,' said Waning.

Jake held his breath, unable to speak, unable to do anything. This had been the point when the last book had proved dangerous, as the hidden spores exploded. Although he knew that they were all protected from whatever may be inside the glass case by the airtight seals, if there were any hazards now exposed, it would delay the proper examination of the book by Michelle for her article.

The green cover, which appeared to be made of some sort of thick card, was turned over, revealing a blank page beneath.

Jake's eyes went to the monitors registering the conditions inside the glass case. No changes. No hazards so far.

He switched his attention back to the CCTV screen with the book in tight close-up. He saw the ends of Waning's gloved fingers delicately touch the blank page, and then lift it and move it gently back, to reveal writing on the next page.

'The first leaf of the book is blank,' said Waning. 'I suspect it is merely an endpaper. Beneath that is a title page, stating . . .'

Jake repeated the words to himself that he saw on the screen as Waning read them out:

'"Physikiana", with a subtitle in Latin which translates as "A treatise on changing physical appearances by magic". The name of the author is given as Roger Bacon.'

'Wow!' Jake heard Michelle gasp beside him.

227

He turned to look at her. She was staring into the lab, at the book inside the glass case, a look of awe on her face. She turned to him, suddenly animated.

'Roger Bacon! This is even better than I'd hoped for!'

'He's good?' As Jake asked the question, he felt stupid. He rummaged around in his memory for things Lauren might have told him about Roger Bacon. He dimly remembered her telling him something about the man, but that had been a long time ago, when they'd first been going out together, and at that time he hadn't paid as much attention to her interest in what were called 'unorthodox sciences' as he should have; he'd been only interested in her: the way she looked, the way she laughed, the way she made him feel.

'You don't know about Roger Bacon?' said Michelle, and there was a note of outraged accusation in her voice.

'Well, I *do*,' said Jake defensively. 'But not as much as I should,' he added lamely.

'Thirteenth-century genius, philosopher and scientist,' said Michelle. 'He taught at Oxford, and in Paris, and elsewhere. He wrote some of the most important works on astronomy and astrology . . .'

'Horoscopes?' queried Jake.

Michelle shook her head.

'Real astrology,' she said. 'Not the crappy fortune-

228

telling stuff you see in the papers. Bacon was the real thing! He wrote the *Opus Maju,* which deals with things like microscopes, telescopes, hydraulics, steam ships, flying machines, long before someone actually produced them!'

More confirmation of Lauren's theory that we'd have been in space hundreds of years before we were, if these books hadn't been hidden, reflected Jake.

'So this book . . .' He gestured towards the observation window, at Lucy Waning slowly turning the pages of the book.

'"Changing physical appearances by magic",' said Michelle, the note of awe still in her voice. 'This is wilder than anything else he ever did, and if Bacon says it's possible, then I bet you it is!'

'So do I, Ms Faure,' said a voice behind them.

Jake whirled round, and found himself looking into the beaming face of Alex Munro. The door had opened so quietly he hadn't heard him come in.

Jake, open-mouthed in shock, stared at Munro. He turned to Michelle, expecting to find her as astonished as he was. Or rather, he expected her to look as if she was wondering who this strange man in the neat dark suit was. But Michelle just looked uncomfortable, and turned away from the bewildered Jake.

'Good to see you again, Jake,' said Munro pleasantly. 'And thank you for bringing us the book.' He gestured at the lab around them. 'We own this facility. Through another company, of course.'

Jake continued to stare at Michelle, who wouldn't look him in the eyes.

'Michelle!' he appealed.

She turned to him, awkward and ashamed.

'Pierce Randall offered me a really good deal,' she said. 'Too good to say no to.'

'A good deal?' echoed Jake, still in a state of shock.

'Money, and a very well-paid job with our public relations department,' said Munro. 'The sort of offer we tried to make to you. But you said no.'

'But . . .' burbled Jake, still stunned. He turned to Michelle and asked: 'When did they offer this to you?'

'Right at the start,' said Michelle. 'Before we even met.'

'So, that business of me being kidnapped, and you finding me . . .'

'Was a set-up,' said Munro. 'You weren't harmed . . .'

'You chloroformed me!' raged Jake.

Munro shrugged.

'A relatively harmless procedure,' he said. 'Our people knew what they were doing. You were never at risk.'

'Oh no? Two men tried to kill me! They were going to shred me up and feed me to pigs!'

Munro shook his head.

'They were nothing to do with us,' he said. 'Why should we do anything like that? We had you where we wanted you. And, if you found a book, you'd bring it here to us. There was no need for any violence on our part.'

'So, who were they? Those men?'

'I don't know,' Munro admitted. 'Competitors, obviously. Possibly mercenaries, hired to get hold of any book you managed to find.' He gave a slight smile. 'Your reputation as someone who finds the lost books of Malichea has spread, Jake. You're becoming quite famous among those who want the hidden library.'

Jake glared at him grimly.

'This book is mine,' he said.

Munro shook his head.

'Officially, the book doesn't exist. So it belongs to whoever has it in their possession. Right now, that's us, Pierce Randall. Our employee, Ms Faure, discovered the book and brought it here.'

'*I* discovered it!' stormed Jake. 'Me and Robert, and a sniffer dog!'

Munro shrugged again.

'That is debatable,' he said. 'Of course, you can always sue us and try and recover the book that way. All you need is a firm of very good solicitors.' He smiled. 'But I would remind you that we at Pierce Randall are the very best.'

231

Munro looked at the CCTV monitors, where Lucy Waning was still turning the pages of the book.

'It appears to be safe from any kind of toxins,' he murmured. He smiled. 'Roger Bacon: "A treatise on changing physical appearances by magic". I can think of many of our clients who would be greatly interested in the information contained in these pages, and would pay very well for it. We might even have an auction for it.'

Raging with fury, Jake moved towards Munro, his hands clenched tightly into fists.

Munro stepped back and called out: 'Security!'

Immediately, two tough-looking men stepped into the room. The room, already cramped, now felt like being inside a small lift.

'I need that book!' snarled Jake. 'I need the knowledge of that book to be made public! I put my life on the line to find it! My friend Robert is near death because of it!'

'And all of that could have been avoided if you'd taken me up on my offer,' said Munro. 'What I will do, Jake, is get the dogs off you. We'll spread the word that we have the book, and you no longer do. The people who are after this book will know that's true, and they'll stop chasing you. You'll be safe.'

'That book is mine!' insisted Jake. 'I found it! It belongs to me!'

'It belonged to the Order of Malichea,' corrected Munro. 'It belongs to whoever takes final possession of it. As our employee, I believe Ms Faure has a very strong claim. I believe, for a start, that it was she who suggested looking at Glastonbury.'

'Yes, but . . .' protested Jake.

'No buts, Jake,' said Munro. 'This meeting is at an end.' Turning to the two security men, he said: 'Escort Mr Wells out of the building. And make sure he doesn't return.'

The two burly men stepped forward and grabbed Jake, and hustled him out of the small room. His last sight was of one of the screens, and Lucy Waning's gloved fingers turning another page of the book.

Chapter 31

Jake stood in front of Gareth's desk in the large imposing office on the third floor of the Department of Science. He was angry, ashamed at being duped by Michelle Faure and Pierce Randall, and deeply guilty over what had happened to Robert. After he'd been escorted from the lab building at Waterloo, part of him had wanted to run away and hide. But that wouldn't help Lauren. He needed to get her back to England. And he wanted revenge against Pierce Randall. And so he'd returned to his office, and asked to see Gareth.

'I'm not even sure why I agreed to see you,' snapped Gareth. 'I should have sacked you. I should have had your pass locked out so you couldn't even get into the building.'

'I can get you Pierce Randall,' said Jake.

Gareth scoffed.

'You can't even keep one tiny book when you get hold of it,' he said. 'And what makes you think we want Pierce Randall?'

'They want the books out there to make money from. You want the books to stay hidden,' said Jake.

Gareth shook his head.

'I told you before all this started, we can live with Pierce Randall,' he said flatly. 'We know their position, they know ours. It's a mutual stand-off. We are not planning on entering into a war with Pierce Randall. It could seriously harm us. We have learnt to live with the status quo, the way things are.'

Jake frowned, puzzled.

'Then why did you agree to see me?' he asked.

'To cut you adrift,' said Gareth. 'And to explain to you personally, why I am doing it. You are a liability, Jake. You've caused more problems that anyone else over the Order of Malichea. I thought that having you in the department would mean we'd be able to keep a watchful eye on you and stop you doing anything stupid. That obviously isn't the case, it seems it only encourages you, despite my firm instructions to you to the contrary.'

'But . . .' began Jake, about to launch a defence; but he was cut short by Gareth's expression: anger — kept in check by Gareth's self-discipline.

'You will be sacked with immediate effect,' Gareth

said. 'You will receive three months' salary as severance. You will not be allowed to work in any government department. If you attempt to publicise the Order of Malichea or the hidden library, you will find yourself in jail.' His eyes became dark gimlets that bored into Jake as he added, in a threatening tone: 'And if you persist, worse may happen to you. Do you understand?'

Numbly, Jake nodded. Gareth's expression softened slightly, and he added, in a quieter voice: 'I will give you one concession. I know why you did what you tried to do, and a part of me is romantic enough to admire someone who tries to do something for the woman he loves.'

What Gareth had just said, and the quiet almost wistful way he said it, staggered Jake.

'We will allow you to make one Skype call to Ms Graham and tell her what has happened; and the fact that you lost the book; and that you have been sacked. We will allow you to make this call without censorship at either end, although it will be monitored. You will also be able to tell her the good news that her cousin has recovered consciousness and will make a full recovery.'

Jake looked at Gareth with relief flooding through him.

'Robert's all right?' he asked, still unsure.

'As all right as anyone can be who's got a fractured skull and was beaten as badly as he was,' said Gareth. 'But, yes. I heard this morning from the hospital with the good news. As for the man you shot . . .'

'I didn't!' protested Jake. Then his eyes dropped and he said, 'It was self-defence.'

'As I understand it, they were trapped inside a car by air bags at the time,' countered Gareth.

'They were going to kill me!' said Jake. 'If I hadn't stopped them coming for me . . .'

'They won't be coming after you again,' said Gareth.

Jake studied him, curious.

'You've had them taken out?' he asked.

'What has happened to them is of no importance to you,' said Gareth.

'It is if they come looking for revenge,' said Jake.

Gareth looked at Jake with the blankest expression Jake had thought he'd ever seen.

'They will not be coming after you,' said Gareth simply. 'Or anyone else.'

So, they are dead, thought Jake.

'And now,' said Gareth, getting to his feet, 'I thought you might like to use my office to make your call to Ms Graham. Much more private than your own.'

Jake looked at the clock.

'It's ten o'clock at night in New Zealand,' he said.

237

'And I believe Ms Graham is at home waiting for your call,' said Gareth. He pointed to his computer on his desk. 'I understand everything is set up and waiting.'

With that, Gareth left the office and closed the door.

Chapter 32

Jake sat at Gareth's desk and looked at Lauren on the screen. Lauren looked back at him, shocked.

'My God, Jake!' she said. 'What's been happening to you?'

'I met some people who didn't agree with me,' said Jake, trying to appear flippant and make light of it, though inside he felt sick and hollow. So much danger, so many risks, Robert nearly dying, and all for nothing.

'Mr Findlay-Weston says we can talk without getting cut off,' she said.

'Yes,' said Jake. 'He sees this as a parting gift.'

Lauren frowned.

'What do you mean?'

'He's sacking me, with immediate effect. He's also warned me off looking for the books.' Then he smiled at her, just to let her know that he wasn't being put

239

off. 'But, that's just a warning. He can't stop me, and he knows it.'

'He can hurt you,' said Lauren.

'He's already hurt me by keeping you there and me here,' said Jake. His tone grew sadder as he said, 'Robert got hurt. Badly hurt. He's in hospital with a fractured skull.'

Lauren gasped, shocked.

'So that's why he hasn't been in touch,' she said. 'I tried emailing him, and phoning him . . .'

'I know, and I should have told you before,' apologised Jake, 'but I was under a lot of pressure.'

'From the people who did that to you?'

'Among others,' said Jake.

As briefly as he could, and aware that their conversation was being monitored, and concerned it could still be cut off, despite Gareth's promises, Jake told Lauren what had happened since they had gone to Glastonbury.

'But you found a book!' said Lauren excitedly.

'Yes,' said Jake. 'Number 557. They exist, Lauren.' He sighed. 'If only I'd kept hold of it.'

'That doesn't matter,' said Lauren. 'What matters is you're alive. We can find another.' Then her excitement faded and she asked: 'Robert . . . ?'

'I'm going to see him as soon as I leave here,' Jake assured her. 'They say he'll recover, but I want to see for myself. Talk to him, let him know what happened.'

'Give him my love,' said Lauren.

'Of course,' said Jake.

Suddenly, in one corner of the screen, appeared a box with the instruction: *This call will terminate in 60 seconds*.

'Looks like Gareth is going back on his promise,' said Jake bitterly.

'Don't let's waste the precious time we've got left taking about Gareth,' said Lauren. 'Or the books.'

'I love you, Lauren!' burst out Jake. 'We will see each other again. Not like this, but together, holding one another . . .'

'I know,' she said. 'I love . . .'

And then the screen went blank.

Jake shouted out, 'It hasn't been sixty seconds!' But there was no response from Janet outside in the outer office, or from Gareth, or from anyone else.

Jake sat, staring at the blank computer screen.

This isn't over, he thought defiantly. Not by a long way. There's a whole library hidden out there, and Lauren and I, we're going to find that library and show it to the world. This isn't the end; it's the beginning.

Want to know what happens next?
Read on for a gripping taster of
LETHAL TARGET . . .

Prologue

The scream echoed through the tunnel and into the cellar room. A man, screaming in fear. Then suddenly the scream was cut off.

The two men in the cellar didn't react; they were concentrating on the equipment on a small metal table: a hypodermic needle and a series of glass phials containing some sort of liquid. The cellar was old, the sandstone and brick walls almost black with age. A metal bed frame had been screwed to the floor. No mattress, just the frame, with thick wire acting as crude springs. Iron manacles dangled from the bars at its head and foot.

The door of the cellar opened and two uniformed men entered, their uniforms army khaki, black jackboots on their feet shining dully in the half-light. Between them they held a naked man. A strip of thick grey tape had been fixed across his mouth to stop him screaming any more. The man looked towards the metal bed frame in the centre of the cellar. He tried to pull back, his eyes bulging with fear, sweat pouring down his face, his bare feet kicking out; but the grip of the men who held him was too strong.

'Put him on it,' said one of the watching men in Russian.

The two uniformed men dragged the prisoner towards the bed frame and pushed him down on to the wire springs. One sat on him, stopping him from moving, while the other fixed the manacles to his wrists and ankles. Then they stepped back.

The man on the bed began to buck and twist, pulling desperately at the manacles, his actions tearing open the skin of his wrists and ankles as they rubbed against the iron.

The man in command picked up the hypodermic needle from the table. He inserted it into one of the glass phials through the opening at the top and drew some of the liquid into the syringe.

'Hold him,' he ordered the two uniformed men, again, in Russian. They moved to the bed frame and pressed their combined weight down on the struggling prisoner, holding him firmly in place. The man pushed the needle deep into the thigh of the hostage and slowly pushed the plunger down until the syringe was empty. Then he stepped back, and nodded to the two men, who instantly released their hold on the prisoner.

The two soldiers retreated to the cellar door, where they stood and waited. All four men kept their eyes on the hostage chained to the bed frame.

One minute passed, then two, then three. Suddenly wisps of smoke began to appear from the pores in the man's skin, tiny at first, then getting denser. The man struggled, his eyes wide in a mixture of pain and fear, his body arching and thrashing. Then a gush of smoke escaped from his nostrils. Smoke was pouring out of the man, through his skin, his scalp, his feet, his arms . . .

There was a sudden silent explosion, intense white flames bursting out through the smoke, coming from inside the man, and the next second the figure on the bed was a heaving mass of fire, the heat and glare making the watching men recoil.

Almost as suddenly as the fire had begun, it stopped, and there was just a cloud of oily smoke, while ashes fell through the bed frame's wire springs to the cellar floor. All that remained of the captive was the hands and feet, still enclosed in the iron manacles, the whites of the bones visible through the scorched flesh.

The other man by the table, who had been silent so far, shook his head.

'The reaction was too slow,' he said in English. 'We need the book.'

'Our people are looking for it as we speak,' replied

the other. He looked at the smouldering pile of ashes and burnt bone. 'This one was too big. I believe the excess fat under his skin caused the slow reaction time.' He nodded thoughtfully, then called an order to the men by the door. 'Bring in the young woman!' To the man next to him, he growled: 'Her flesh should burn faster.'

Chapter 1

Jake was worried; very worried. He walked around the supermarket, filling up his trolley with his week's supplies, moving on automatic pilot. All he could think of was Lauren. It had been five days since he'd last spoken to her, and that had been by phone, not even Skype, so he hadn't had the chance to see how she looked. She'd sounded odd. Nervous. He knew she couldn't say why, their conversations were monitored by the intelligence services, but usually they found a way to drop a hint if something was worrying one of them, so they could read between the lines, put together the clues in texts and phone calls. But this last time, no hint, just an awareness in Jake that something was troubling Lauren. And since that last phone call, nothing. No texts, no emails, no phone calls, no letters.

It was at times like this he felt the distance between them: her in New Zealand and him in London.

The previous night, when it was daytime in New Zealand, he'd even phoned the place where she worked, the Antarctic Survey Research Centre in Wellington, in case something had happened to her, a serious accident, and she wasn't able to make contact with him. But the woman he'd spoken to had said Samantha Adams (Lauren's cover name in New Zealand) hadn't been in to work for four days, and they hadn't heard from her, which was very unusual.

They'd been in touch with Lauren's flatmate, a young woman called Kristal, who said that Lauren had told her she was going away for a day or so, and not to worry. So she hadn't. But since the Survey Research Centre had got in touch, Kristal had contacted the local police and hospitals to see if there had been any reports of unidentified young women having been in an accident; but there had been nothing.

'We're very worried about her,' the woman told Jake. 'This is so unlike her. If you hear from her, would you ask her to get in touch with us?'

Jake promised he would. Just as he was about to ring off, the woman asked him if Samantha had any Russian connections.

'Russian connections?' Jake frowned.

'It's just that on the last day she was in the office she had a call from someone, and the switchboard operator was fairly sure the person was Russian.'

'A man or a woman?'

'A man.'

A Russian? Jake was puzzled. Lauren had never mentioned knowing any Russians. But then, it had been five months since they'd last seen one another. Anything could have happened in that time. What was clear was that Lauren seemed to have vanished suddenly, and without trace . . .